Standing Stillbury

and

Concrete Hardening

Standing Stillbury and Concrete Hardening

David Everington

A SQUARE ONE PUBLICATION

First published in 1996 by
Square One Publications,
The Tudor House
Upton upon Severn, Worcs. WR8 0HT

British Library Cataloguing in Publication Data

*Typeset in 11pt Baskerville by Avon Dataset Ltd,
Bidford-on-Avon, B50 4JH
Printed by Antony Rowe Ltd, Chippenham, Wilts*

Contents

Preface

Although many of my life's experiences have been gained from a modest role in the public affairs of both Shrewbury and Telford, none of the characters described in this book represents a real person from those places. For obvious reasons, the story has to have people like town clerks, mayors, council chairmen and chief executives, members of Parliament, company chairmen etc. since the sort of people who hold those offices would usually be involved in the circumstances upon which this fiction is based.

Standing Stillbury and Concrete Hardening, though in parts (and perhaps rather obviously) inspired by Shrewsbury and Telford are just examples of how two different places might approach the same situation. I have nowhere else from which to draw the background upon which this story is painted. I have, it must be admitted, visited both Oswestry and Milton Keynes in recent years but could make neither head nor tail of either.

If there are lessons to be learned form the story, then they might be applicable to a score or more places remaining in the shires of England where the attitudes found in 'Standing Stillbury' hold sway – though I doubt if any single town would provide a complete match with either Standing Stillbury or Concrete Hardening. As far as I know, neither Blanks Bearing nor Zugswang Components exist anywhere either.

In essence, the following pages attempt a critical, humorous and yet affectionate look at a certain type of English town, coupled with a serious point about the need to look to the future.

David Everington
Shrewsbury
July 1996

Foreword

Standing Stillbury is a beautiful town with a long history. It is almost surrounded by a slow-moving, sweet-water river. The one gap in this natural barrier has, for many centuries, been guarded by a splendid castle. The ancient borough has a magnificent abbey, a public school, its very own town drunk (a gentleman so dedicated to his calling that he enjoys considerable public recognition of his status) and is the centre of county government. On each road into Standing Stillbury is a peeling and faded sign which tells you this is a mediaeval town – a piece of information which is correct.

The choice of the site within the river loop and the building of the castle were thought necessary in a once turbulent borderland. Although these things contribute much to the Town's present splendour, they didn't achieve their historic purpose. The result of the only serious attack was immediate surrender by the burgesses lest trade and their grand houses be damaged and they themselves hanged for their troublesomeness. However, the river and the castle do seem to have had their intended effect so far as new ideas are concerned.

Thus, a great deal of talking is done in Standing Stillbury. But change is first resisted and then, if it must happen, undertaken with great reluctance and even acrimony. It is the sort of place where a Church built in the 16th century would still be known as The New Church, to distinguish it from the one next door built in the 14th. And at one time there were nearly as many churches as there are public houses. Even now there are quite a few churches, some still in use for their intended purpose.

There is a town football team – known as The Stills – which hovers year after year in the lower depths of the Football League. Every few seasons a new manager is appointed and he assures the Town that, provided 'the lads' play to their full potential, and don't have bad luck with injuries, there is no reason why they shouldn't manage the occasional home win. 'The lads', it must be said, often having been bought at half-price and past their sell-by-date from football clubs in distant, large cities, are sometimes older than the Manager.

The Stills are sustained by the gate money from small crowds of townsfolk and a few hill-farmers from over the old border who, between them, number about one tenth of those claiming to be active supporters. The title 'active supporter' is claimed by anyone who attended a match at least once during the ten years immediately preceding the claim. The Team once reached the final of a minor football competition designed to give a brief moment of fame to clubs from the lower depths of the game. A competition was organised to produce an anthem to be sung by the supporters at the great event, in the Capital. Typically, it was entered by more Standing Stillb'rians then ever attended their side's home matches.

The nice thing about the Stills is that their's was the last football ground in England where the home crowd politely applauded a good away goal. But in contrast to this small courtesy, after every home defeat, a number of those present, red-faced and fuming, storms out of the ground declaring 'That's it for me. I'm finished! They're not worth bloody watching. They don't soddin' WANT to go up. The friggin' directors are useless. That's the last time I set foot in this effing ground.' They all turn up again two weeks later.

This particular group remembers fondly the days of the Great Arturo, an Italian immigrant of past years who enjoyed the Indian summer of his career with The Stills. He gave them their time of glory by smashing in goals which took the net off the posts, spraying passes which he could land on a sixpenny piece from fifty yards and actually scoring more than anyone ever had before.

The arrival of the Great Arturo was the best thing that ever happened to Standing Stillbury. He still lives in the area, in contentment I hope, though getting older and more forgotten as the years pass. He could probably get into the team today.

Despite everything, the old Town is regarded with pride and affection – and so it should be. Its people get a great sense of enjoyment from a weekend stroll through narrow streets which still have some interesting shops owned by local families. Some of them sell antiques, second-hand books, curios, stamps, coins and medals for collectors, wine, fishing tackle and other similar things of interest which can't make enough profit to pay the rents in sterilised modern shopping malls.

If you were born in Standing Stillbury and have re-mained, you are very lucky. The Town gives you an almost touchable and smellable sense of continuity, stretching far back to a wretched and blood-stained Saxon past. You can pass your life and die there, quite without lost content, having left your word on one of the pages of a nicely bound book with much still to be written. Some people, to be sure, fret about how big a word they will be leaving, not realising how little that matters when measured against the long run.

Those who are prosperous, secure, literate and even a little cultured, enjoy Standing Stillbury especially. It is their sort of place: a town of tweed jackets, tidily combed hair, brown brogues and a pipeful of Borkum Riff. The men, on the other hand, generally dress a bit more stylishly.

Standing Stillbury had for centuries, until very recent times, outshone all the other nearby towns in size and im-portance. The fact that it did so was the very essence of its identity. But now, the councillors and some of the towns-people get a bit upset about Concrete Hardening.

Concrete Hardening used to be a messy collection of dingy, small towns and villages at the forgotten back-end of the County, Deepshire. You drove through it, holding your nose in warm weather, on the way to somewhere else. These days the small towns and villages are joined together as one single town, growing rapidly and already much bigger and more important than Standing Stillbury – and the Town Council is controlled by grade-A roll-your-own socialists, some of whom neither wear ties nor get their hair cut for ceremonial occasions. They have declared the Town a nuclear-free zone, to the intense relief of its citizens, who consequently sleep more easily in their beds. Like Standing Stillbury, Concrete Hardening is a beautiful place, but in quite a different sort of way.

Perhaps the only thing the two towns agree about is the virtue of preserving trees. But any tree in either town which obstructs a development by the Council is immediately deemed by the Parks Superintendent to be diseased, rotten inside and in imminent danger of falling over on to some passing ratepayer. The workmen come with chainsaws. The usual crowd of idlers and layabouts assembles to watch the tree come down and then casually inspects the sawn cross-section for evidence of the dangerous rot. The strange thing is, you can never see any. But it must be so as the Parks Superintendent has said so and HE KNOWS. It's quite amazing how often trees in the way of council development are found to be rotten and a danger to the public.

This never happens with trees on private property, no matter how their owners plead for permission to chop them down. THEY are always decreed to be both sound and a blessing of nature which the community is entitled to share. Sometimes they fall down and crush the landowner's new car just a week or so after having been preserved by formal order of the Council.

In Concrete Hardening there is less talk and more action. Things often happen quickly there. It deserves to be regarded with admiration. It will eventually keep many of the comfortable people of Standing Stillbury in well-paid jobs from which they will come home in the evenings and at weekends to enjoy pleasant and prosperous lives, reflecting upon their good fortune to work in the one town and live in the other.

The people of Concrete Hardening don't get upset about Standing Stillbury because their town has no ancient status to be lost to another: it is visibly successful and without that slight preciousness about itself which will, one supposes, come with the fullness of time.

However, one of the small, old towns which is now just a minor part of Concrete Hardening, Lower Middle Sniffley, cannot come to terms with that fact. Lower Middle Snifflies (as they are known) often look back sadly, and even angrily, to the days when they were quite separate from all the new housing estates and factories with which they have become inextricably linked.

They have a minor public school and an ancient, cheerful market – and a famous poet once lived there as well. Unfortunately, the poet seemed only to have unkind things to say about Lower Middle Sniffley – so those few residents who have heard of him (or, indeed, of any other poet) don't mention him much.

Lower Middle Sniffley also has a rogue branch of the Cats' Protection League which has devised a training programme whereby their fetid felines learn to sniff hardening concrete at 250 yards. They then rush to dance moonlight quadrilles over it, leaving trails of pug-marks to be discovered by the owners the next morning. Being sniffy about hardening concrete is Lower Middle Sniffley's main contribution to Concrete Hardening.

Standing Stillbury and Concrete Hardening, though very different, are the two largest towns in Deepshire -where the pattern of life in some parts has hardly changed in centuries. Some of the land in the County has been owned by the same families since the middle ages. Indeed, ancient land ownerships have given rise to the humorous anecdote that Deepshire is twice as big as itself – there being at least four great landowners, for example Lord Pratford, who are routinely referred to as 'owning half the County'.

Going to London on business from Deepshire is still a notable event – even more so since the Railway Company, aided by a cynical government and the still-unexplained acquiescence of the Tory Members of Parliament, severed the direct rail connection with London which the Shire had enjoyed since the earliest days of rail transport.

The events of the county are chronicled each day by BBC Radio Deepshire and the evening newspaper, the Deepshire Planet. They both report, for the most part quite gently, upon the village fetes and WI meetings and the public and private scandals which mark one month from another in our lives.

Each Spring they find some kind of motor vehicle which

cannot be moved because a bird has nested in it. A black and white photograph will show a group of carefully chosen rustics examining the stricken vehicle with a nicely posed mixture of humour and dismay.

At each May-time election of a local council they discover, with annually renewed astonishment, a family which has received a voting card for a one-year-old child or even their mongrel dog – implying, with more joviality than malice, that the council staff who issue the cards must be a halfpenny short of a shilling. They enjoy sharing the joke with us and are too polite to point out that this sort of thing only happens because some idiot or publicity-seeker in the family must have put the baby's or the dog's name on the electoral register form in the first place. Once the elections are over, and the Summer gets hot, media attention switches to blue-green algae, with dire warnings of what it might do if ingested by people paddling in ponds and pools.

Every Winter, Deepshire County Council has a financial crisis of apocalyptic proportions when the Government is said not to be stumping up enough money to keep more then half the schools and two fire stations going. By the following Summer the schools and the fire stations are mostly still there, as they always have been. One day, I suppose, it really will be true and we won't have believed them when it mattered. It seems odd for Deepshire County Council to have financial difficulties of this kind – it having long since abandoned any dependency upon money and gone over to an alternative means of exchange known as 'resources' – a word which can be slipped into a report to a committee with much less impact upon the sensibilities of members and their electors than if cash itself were mentioned.

As a matter of fact, a much greater threat to the future of Deepshire's schools is posed by snow. It is difficult to explain this to those who haven't been living in the Shire for a long time. In the rotten Winter of 19– when the River Septon got so heavily iced-up that you could drive a motor car on it – and someone actually did – hardly any schools closed at all.

Since then, every successive Winter has witnessed the phenomenon of smaller and smaller amounts of snow causing the closure of greater and greater numbers of Deepshire's schools, some of which are located near to businesses all of which remain open. If this effect were extrapolated on a carefully constructed graph, it would indicate that by the next century, a quarter of an inch of snow will result in the immediate closure of 95% of Deepshire's schools, and the mere threat of it at least 50% of them. No-one has yet explained the dynamics of this inexorable process which loosely resembles the chain reaction consequent upon atomic fission. The net result, though, has been extraordinary. Children who once rushed out to enjoy the snow before lessons now crowd anxiously around wireless sets to hear if Radio Deepshire has added the name of their school to the blessed list of snow-time closures – and the telephone calls announcing the closures to the radio station land, at their peak, thicker than the offending flakes.

The County Council was once the preserve of Deepshire's landed classes – a sort of country gentleman's club in the County Town where the polite and deferential clerks were the equivalent of the waiters at Boodle's or White's – serving reports and memos instead of brandies with soda. (Yes – I know. In the cases two particular county aldermen they had to serve up memos WITH brandy and soda, but those days are long-gone)

The magnificent oil-portraits of such gentry as served in the Chairmanship stretch far along the corridors into another century and another world. Those of the most distant past appear to have struck such dignified, superior and awe-inspiring poses that one might think they couldn't possibly have had to endure natural bodily functions like the rest of us.

These days, the County, like Concrete Hardening (and to a great extent because of it) is run by Socialists. Departmental Chief Officers are less likely to fit the traditional grandee mould and one was recently seen in public wearing an anorak. The country gents' club atmosphere has blown away and in its place is professionalism, earnestness, industriousness, considerable brain-power and ... political correctness. Committees now have 'chairs', sexual harassment has been banned (to the intense ire of at least three secretaries who joined up in order to enjoy some) and every kind of prescribed employment quota has been fulfilled with enthusiasm – for the disabled, ethnic minorities, Seventh-Day-Adventists, gays and lesbians etc. Indeed, the County Council has evidently anticipated a piece of future legislation and employed a more or less pro-rata number of Deepshire's oddballs and eccentrics. Of course, in order to achieve this last objective they had to REDUCE the number to the present figure of about two per department ...

For all that, Deepshire County Council doesn't do a bad job and deserves credit for keeping the main roads in reasonable repair, mending the bridges and producing what is called a structure plan for the County. Everyone agrees with the Structure Plan until he or she wants to undertake some development which doesn't fit into it – in which case they disagree with it. The enthusiastic Tourism Department is always willing to send a nymphomation pack and recently lured an American family to visit the County. They came from Kansas and thought it was quite nice though rather small.

Each evening in the week the radio station gives the price per kilo fetched by the various types of farm animal in the livestock markets dotted throughout the Shire. Soon, I expect, they will interview the old man from Lower Middle Sniffley who remembers the historic day, many years ago, when the motorway which probes into Deepshire as far as Concrete Hardening, was entirely free of orange and white plastic cones. They ought to do this before he dies and the memory with him.

There isn't much excitement. At one time people started making political protests by hi-jacking airliners to Havana. Last year in Deepshire a disturbed young man hi-jacked a mini-bus full of old ladies and made the driver take him to Steeple-Nicely.

Once there, he handed his fake gun over to the policeman who, breathing heavily and sweating profusely, had

pursued the bus by bicycle all the way from Standing Stillbury. Most of the old ladies had been so deeply immersed
in conversations, one with another, that they remain, to this
day, quite unaware of what had happened.

Chapter 1 – A Problem

The Town Clerk, Mr Muffle, the Mayor, Fred Meadows, and the Member of Parliament, Jack Fudge, sat glumly in the Mayor's Parlour. It was at the front of the Town Hall, an imposing free-standing town house of the mid-1700s. The first Earl of Deepshire had built it for those times when he was forced, against his will, to leave his country estates for business in Standing Stillbury, the County Town.

There was a slight vulgarity about the grand front-door. It was surmounted by a portico, bearing the Earl's coat of arms. The coat of arms was maintained in pristine colours and the portico was supported by two pairs of Doric columns. The Earl had reasoned that, if he had to visit this wretched town of scavenging lawyers, stone-faced merchants and bent-backed clerks, then they would be made to understand just how rich he was. (At the time of the Earl's decision to build the house there were no estate agents or accountants by those names or he might have included them in his thoughts as well.) The vanity which had motivated the Earl in constructing such a house could also be ascribed to the size and architectural detail of others, some older, some newer, peppered here and there throughout the Town.

After more than two centuries, the Earl of Deepshire's house still looked very fine indeed, despite having long-since been sold for use as the Town Hall. There had been a bit of window tax avoidance at ground-floor level but the house remained cool in Summer and tolerably warm in Winter, made more cosy by the retention of coal fires in each of the rooms presently used as offices.

All through Winter the coal had to be carried to each room, twice every day, by the elderly caretaker, Mr Mondelski. He was a jovial Polish war veteran, one of those who had been imprisoned by the Russians after their treacherous seizure of his country, jointly with the Germans. Then, when the Germans attacked the Russians in their turn, he, and the others who hadn't been murdered, had been grudgingly released to join the Free Polish forces in Britain. He had never wanted to go back home.

Mr Mondelski's appointment as caretaker in the 1940s, in preference to locally-born applicants, had caused outrage amongst the lower-deck, saloon-bar lawyers of which the Town had always possessed a large number. It was all heavily reported in the local newspaper. But the Town Clerk of that time, a man of considerable standing and principle, had sharply reminded Standing Stillbury that Mr Mondelski came from Poland and had fought on our side in the late war. This point eventually met with ill-graced acceptance and the matter was slowly forgotten. Few Standing Stillb'rians knew exactly where Poland was. But they realised it wasn't Germany and therefore couldn't be all that bad.

But now Mr Mondelski was older, his hair thinning into silvery-grey strands. As each year passed he got a bit less jovial and a bit more grumbly. Carrying the coal was a burden as there were three floors – the highest divided into smallish rooms with low ceilings. They had been bedrooms for domestic servants but were now occupied by the Committee Clerks. There was no lift.

The Mayor, Aldermen and Burgesses of Standing Stillbury, the splendid collective name taken by the Councillors, had noticed that Mr Mondelski found the coal carrying more difficult with each passing year. They were not totally insensitive and did notice things like this. Since they had all got to like Mr Mondelski, a feeling had developed that central heating would have to be installed one day, when the budget would allow it. That would be difficult however. The Mayor Aldermen and Burgesses were quite dedicated to their appointed task of keeping the Borough rates as low as possible. They had been elected by a citizenry, each member of which bitterly resented any public spending unless it was to repair the hole in the road outside his or her own particular house.

The Borough Treasurer, Mr Tite, who also quite liked

him, nevertheless wondered if Mr Mondelski's heart attack wouldn't come first. Then a younger man could be appointed and he could carry the coals for a few more financial years. Mr Tite was a naturally very cautious man in financial matters. This could have disadvantages but he wasn't, as far as is known, the sort of Borough Treasurer who placed council money with the Bank of Credit and Commerce International or anything of that sort. He had carefully preserved the wire-stemmed poppy he had bought in 1948 and took it out of the old tobacco tin in which he kept it, in a desk drawer, as Remembrance Sunday approached each November.

The old house itself was occupied by the Town Clerk, Mr Muffle, and his own departmental staff who were the Council's solicitors and legal clerks – and the committee clerks in their top-floor garrets. Though many others laid claim to the position, the committee clerks were the hub of the council's affairs. They produced the agendas for the meetings of the council and its many committees, they recorded the decisions taken and they badgered and chased the staff of all the other departments to do the bidding of the elected members. They formed the only group of people through whose hands all decisions of the council passed.

The Borough Treasurer, the Borough Surveyor and all their staff were consigned to similarly old buildings, also converted to offices, which had once been the stables and outhouses. Other council departments were dotted around the Town in the brown linoleum-floored rooms of decaying, large former houses, randomly acquired for the purpose over a century or more.

The Mayor's Parlour, on the ground floor, was oak panelled, dark-blue carpeted and badly lit. This gave an added sharpness to the view through the tall sash window which faced down the slope of Grout Street towards the Bear Hotel at the far end. The famous golden bear could be seen clearly, over the doorway. Halfway down Grout Street, a crude cardboard sign, badly written with a black felt marker and placed at the entrance to an alley – and Standing Stillbury was famous for its alleyways – indicated that 'continental beer garden' was to be found somewhere at the rear. The sign didn't impart much hope.

They were all three in their mid-fifties and dressed in dark suits crumpled by a day in committee rooms. Similar meetings between similar sorts of people had been held in this room for many decades.

The Mayor had a florid, red-veined face, marked by the official engagements and free gin-and-tonics of a solid half year in his ancient office. He balanced heavy, dark-framed spectacles half-way along a rather wide nose. He tended to look over the top of the glasses when he spoke. He thought it added to the gravity of his appearance. He was five feet six inches tall and thick around the waist.

In real life he was the proprietor of a corner shop with an off-licence and a news agency. He was Mayor because he had stayed on the Council long enough for his turn to come around. If you did that, you got to be Mayor however stupid or clever you were and whatever your political party, if any. Other councillors, whatever their politics, faithfully voted for you to enjoy your year in office. Even those councillors who had heaped odium and abuse upon the new incumbent in the council chamber the previous week would happily support the proposal that he take the mayoral robes, splendidly red and lined with ermine, and, in the process, make generous, laudatory speeches about him.

This little, wheel-oiling hypocrisy always charmed the ladies of the new mayoral family, and their near relatives, who would arrive at the annual mayor-making ceremony in their floral frocks and best hats, convinced they were VIP guests at an event of enormous importance. The remaining 99.9% of the townspeople would hardly be aware of anything taking place at all and, if asked the name of the Mayor, would think for a while, scratch their heads, and usually come up with no answer or that of one who, they vaguely recalled, had held that office a year or so before.

But despite this you did, in a modest sort of way, scratch a small mark on the slate of local history if you got to be Mayor. Your name would be added to the list of Mayors of Standing Stillbury which had been carefully preserved and maintained since the very first one, appointed when the Mayoralty was created by Royal Charter in 16–. The slowly expanding list was always re-printed in the annual council yearbook and, even if you had long-since retired from the Council, the elected members of the day and the Town Clerk would always attend your funeral. The report of your demise, in the Deepshire Planet, would make much of that ephemeral year in office long before. Even if you had since won the Nobel Prize for physics or written a best-selling history of Albania (neither occurrence having been frequent, it must be confessed) it would always be headlined 'DEATH OF EX-MAYOR'.

The Committee Clerks, who had to arrange the annual mayor-making ceremony, were much less impressed than the guests, having seen it too often before. At the end of the celebratory luncheon, which became meaner in content with the financial strictures of each passing year, they would sneak off to the nearest pub and exchange views on the likely performance of the newly-elected for his term of office. Sometimes their assessments were flattering, sometimes not. But even they acknowledged that very few Mayors of Standing Stillbury had ever made a hash of the job. There were the Town Clerk and a dedicated Mayor's Officer to steer them through their year and the most unlikely people usually grew into it, more or less. This was just as well because some pretty unlikely people did get to be Mayor of Standing Stillbury.

But Fred Meadows, the Mayor in this year of 19–, was a lot better than average. He was an able wheeler-dealer in small town politics who didn't offend too many people too often and who, like most of his council colleagues, had a vague notion that his job was to keep the town much as it was and always had been. He drank a little too much, but seldom beyond the bounds of acceptable social behaviour. And he had a great and unusual quality: sometimes, just sometimes, he asked himself whether a decision would be good for the Town before wondering how it related to the official doctrines of his party.

On the Sunday following the mayor-making ceremony, a splendid service for the new holder of that office would be held at the magnificent civic church of Standing Stillbury, St. Suter the Martyr's – St Suter having been a mediaeval municipal reformer whose body, still bearing the fatal stab wounds in the back, was miraculously preserved in a nearby mausoleum.

On each seat there would be placed a card which announced that it was reserved for councillors, senior officials and their guests. The regular week-in, week-out worshippers would be kept out until these had all been seated. The Church authorities refused to take part in the forcible interception of their own congregation for this purpose. They pretended that it didn't happen and insisted that instead the Council provide hapless junior clerks, dragooned against their will for the purpose, to stand guard at the door. When complained to later by their indignant parishioners they would express much surprise at such an outrage and undertake to look into it, every year. In this, of course, they were being ecumenical with the truth.

The Member of Parliament of many years standing, Jack Fudge, had a narrow sharply chiselled sort of face, above which receding, intensely dark hair was combed backwards like some parody of a wartime advertisement for Brylcream. His hair had retained its colour so well that some unkind people, in his own party and others, occasionally suggested that he had achieved this by artificial means. This however was untrue. Some claims to the discredit of Jack Fudge were well justified but not, as it happened, this one. Like most parliamentarians of his age, he also drank a little more than was good for him but, like the Mayor, he seemed to keep it under control.

Jack Fudge was taller than the Mayor. Unlike him, he was not a native of Standing Stillbury. Members of Parliament are very seldom local people. There is a perversity which makes it almost impossible for the members of constituency parties to agree upon a locally-born parliamentary candidate, however good he or she might be. Local party-members, by their nature, are known too well and have enemies as well as friends. So their candidature always provokes bitter in-fighting, mostly kept beneath the surface, after which the party selection committee interviews a series of nonentities and hopefuls from anywhere but their own town. They then settle for a complete unknown who speaks well and has a presentable wife, or conversely, a husband of sound background and no convictions for child-molesting. In the case of the Conservative Party, in Standing Stillbury and a couple of score other places, the candidate also has to promise solemnly to campaign in Parliament to bring back hanging and flogging. If elected, he gleefully takes his seat and usually forgets that particular promise.

Jack Fudge's strange views on a number of issues had resulted in his being known as Daft Jack. This was only behind his back, of course. But, though some described him as a man of many hidden shallows, he wasn't at all daft. It was, after all, he and no-one else who had got to be Member of Parliament for Standing Stillbury, one of the safest and nicest seats in England. He was set up for life. There was nothing daft about that and, in truth, he deserved praise for the taste he had displayed in choosing a constituency.

The Town Clerk, Mr Muffle, six feet tall, also thin-faced but rather studious in appearance (a point exaggerated by his thin-framed but thick-lensed glasses) normally drank very little. He, like the Mayor, was a native of the Town. He counted himself immensely lucky to have risen through the Council's ranks to the top job: the Town Clerk being, in effect, the Chief Executive. He so enjoyed life in Standing Stillbury that he sometimes admitted to himself that he would have stayed, even as a junior solicitor. A transitory manager of the Town's football club – The Stills – had once described Standing Stillbury as a graveyard of ambition – and meant it as a compliment. Mr Muffle, who happened to be a loyal though despairing supporter of The Stills, agreed and was well aware that to live in such a town with the advantages of his position was a very happy circumstance.

His problem was a streak of restlessness which sometimes made him want to make things happen. Nothing outlandish, of course. Just a bit of progress here and there; an occasional polite doffing of the Town's cap to the fact that, even in Standing Stillbury, one century occasionally passed into another. He was acutely aware that, in the company his chosen career caused him to keep, this inclination often had to be kept firmly bottled.

The Mayor, the Member of Parliament and the Town Clerk each had a large tumbler of Scotch from which he sipped frequently, almost anxiously. The Scotch had been poured from a bottle kept in the Mayoral drinks cabinet, one of antique design which fitted into the corner of the room and had a conch-shell design inlaid in the oak door. The cabinet was normally kept locked against raids by the more adventurous Town Hall staff – or more specifically by Mr Muffle's unmarried secretary, Miss Peeves. Miss Peeves drank anything within reach at those moments when she became convinced, quite rightly, of the futility of her life. At the time of this story that was about twice each week. She was, after all, going through the protopause, that tense and anxious forty-or-so years endured by all women before they reach the menopause.

Most large public organisations, and many private ones, have a Miss Peeves figure in a secretarial job at the centre of power. They are dedicated, intelligent, and often jealously possessive of their boss, to whom they offer fierce protection from contamination by two categories of people: those perceived to lack importance and those known to disagree with him. They carry real power within an organisation but are themselves sucked dry through a lifetime of thankless service to successive town clerks, borough treasurers or managing directors. Then they are discarded mercilessly at 60 with an ornamental clock and a small pension, to live on to 75 or so, confined to a council flat in some cheerless suburb.

Having brushed shoulders with important and self-important people for most of their careers, they don't feel quite at one with the plebeian herd which lives in the cheerless suburb. So they tend to keep to themselves with a few memories, increasingly muddled, and a bottle of gin, increasingly replaced.

It was late afternoon on a warm June day and people from the nearby offices and shops were starting to leave for home. Many of them walked, since the ancient, pinched roads in Standing Stillbury were so clogged-up with traffic that it was quicker to walk than drive. The bank clerks, such as still had jobs in that once respected but rapidly shrinking profession, the secretaries and the shop assistants, all seemed to scurry, carrying plastic bags full of shopping.

Many of the lawyers, accountants and architects lived in the old houses in or close to the town centre, or in Frankland, just over the toll-bridge. They strolled home more casually, with a sense of ease and enjoyment of the pleasant views which the town afforded to those with the eyes to see. Their shopping would have been done by career-less wives who would be ready to greet them on their return, perhaps with a gin and tonic ready poured, chilled and with a thin slice of lemon or lime. I am afraid that some of the wives would already have enjoyed several of these during the course of the day.

Every few years, one of this latter group, the professional classes if you like, would scandalise Standing Stillbury by falling into disgrace and even getting sent to prison for some gross breach of professional rules or mis-use of his clients' or his partners' money. The miscreants always poured out heart-rending tales of personal tragedy, sadness and hardship which seemed oddly at variance with the perceived joie-de-vivre of their lifestyles before they were found out. It never made any difference. There was still, just, enough resolve amongst the professional bodies and the courts to understand that they had to be severe – if only to convince the handsomely-paying public that the rest of the profession could be trusted with its affairs and its money and that the event was but a unique aberration, never to be repeated. About two years later, on average, it would be.

Sometimes the offender seemed to have salted away enough money to survive. But once the story appeared on the front page of the Deepshire Planet, often couched in regretful and almost apologetic terms, he and his immediate family would soon feel the cold frowns of the Town – most severely from those doing the same thing but not yet caught. A few friends would remain true to them but they would lose the urge to be seen at the Civic Ball, the Round Table Ladies' Night or the Golf Club Dinner.

And in Standing Stillbury an affair of this kind left its stain forever. The offender might live for decades more and even re-establish some kind of position, but the collective memory of the Town would never lose its awareness of that lapse. Nothing much would ever be said, but it would always be there. In fact, the hopelessness of achieving full social redemption usually led the wretch to move somewhere far away after a while.

Those who were discovered having extra-marital affairs, or who left their wives and took up with someone else's, didn't have quite the same problem. There would be private anguish and lasting grief but, after the first flurry of gossip, that sort of thing went almost unremarked in the public domain of Standing Stillbury by the time of these events. In a way this was strange since the situation was almost precisely reversed in national politics at the time: sexual scandal meant automatic ruin whilst charges of thievery and corruption would be blandly brushed aside and might even be followed by promotion to some senior office of state. This, though, was fairly typical of Standing Stillbury. The Town was like an island in a vast ocean where time had done what its name implied.

Soon, the nearby buildings, many constructed in the centuries-old timber-framed style for which Standing Stillbury was famous, would be empty. The street would become almost lifeless but for parties of foreign visitors being taken on conducted tours by the keen, boy-scoutish town guides. I would exempt Henry from the description boy-scoutish, of course. Henry's is not the sort of voice you get at the end of the 'dial a prayer' 'phoneline. The guides would explain this or that piece of local history, of which Standing Stillbury had much. The foreign visitors would politely pretend to understand it all, though really quite bemused.

Then, several hours later when the pubs were emptying, groups of beer-sodden young men would lurch along, shouting abuse at passers-by and one another. (it must be admitted, in the cause of equality, that these days some of the girls can match them in volume, obscenity and menace.) They would remove things which could be broken off cars parked at the street edges. Sometimes they removed the whole car. The police mostly walked around in pairs, especially on Friday and Saturday nights, overwhelmed by the numbers. They had long-since been prevented by the police-hating, all-souls-can-be-redeemed and sociologist classes from saving themselves paperwork and the Town a lot of trouble by giving an exemplary thick-ear to the most aggressive young drunks.

The police, for their part, attracted little sympathy. In a town the size of Standing Stillbury, anyone of any substance who thwarted them would be sure, eventually, to be caught out driving over the alcohol limit or, in the case of the Town's four or five tee-totallers, to be stopped for some minor breach of the road traffic acts. The endless clauses of the road traffic acts gave limitless scope for the quiet settlement of scores or the brightening of an otherwise boring day for the occasional social inadequate who got through the net and acquired a blue uniform.

But, just occasionally, one or two of the drunken, maladjusted young would practically force the police to haul them in and charge them, after committing some particularly serious offence – perhaps an un-provoked life-threatening assault or the killing of a pedestrian whilst, high on drugs or alcohol, driving a stolen car.

They would punch, kick and bite the arresting officers as viciously as they could, until subdued, and then appear in court with a defending solicitor, paid for from public funds, who would movingly describe the tragedy of their early lives and the deep remorse they felt for their foolish actions. It was quite remarkable that the remorse only ever came AFTER arrest. There was no instance on record in Standing Stillbury of an offender walking into a police-station and expressing remorse for something for which he had NOT yet been caught. Remorse appeared to be a post-arrest syndrome in all cases. In some cases you almost got the feeling that the defending solicitor had quietly recommended a course of remorse therapy, frequently lasting through the whole of the court proceedings.

Quite often, the solicitor was so convincing that the defendant would get off or, if conviction was quite unavoidable, he might be sentenced to a period of community service which left ample free time for further wrong-doing. The most serious cases would be taken for foreign holidays with earnest social workers – the sort who believed that only the illiterate could benefit from longer sentences. They always hoped to re-mould their defective characters – the characters of the offenders, that is. The usual result was immediate re-offending upon arrival at their holiday destination and more of the same on their return to Standing Stillbury – but there was a general consensus that the Town would at least have enjoyed a break from their villainy during the period of attempted re-habilitation. (I mean by this a break from the villainy of the offender, not from that of the social worker)

Occasionally, some spirited member of the public would robustly and successfully defend himself from late-night thuggery in the street or physically resist the burglary of his house or the theft of his car. These actions, in stark contrast to those of the yob and criminal classes, were always subjected to the deepest and most enduring scrutiny lest any impression be given that people might be in danger of TAKING THE LAW INTO THEIR OWN HANDS – a possibility which seemed to terrify the police more than crime itself.

But for the constraints upon the police, and the coarse insults they had to endure, the scene would have been similar a hundred or two hundred years before, without the cars of course. However, none of that changed the essential fact that Standing Stillbury, for most of the time, was a town which pleased all who lived there and walked its ancient streets.

But the next couple of hours in the Mayor's Parlour were going to be difficult. The problem was a new vehicle component factory which, the Town Clerk and the other two knew, in strict confidence, was to be built somewhere in England. Deepshire was one of the areas being considered. They didn't know whose factory it would be, or precisely where the company came from, although it was rumoured to be German.

But there might be 500 new jobs and as many more would spring up like mushrooms with smaller local companies who would supply various bits of the components and all sorts of other things such as stationery, canteen supplies, drinks vending machines, bottles of milk, newspapers and office and window cleaning services. All in all, it was a nice lot of employment and extra wages to circulate around the Town. Standing Stillbury might be a contender to have the new factory – but so would Concrete Hardening be, just ten miles away.

The Mayor turned his head away from the scene in the street and peered at the other two, over the top of his glasses. He was slightly agitated and that always made things awkward for the Town Clerk. Mr Muffle didn't like agitation and had built a successful career upon its suppression. You could go a long way in local government if you could suppress agitation firmly. And besides, he had a royal visit on the way. That would generate enough agitation as it was.

Mr Muffle had already explained patiently to the Mayor and the Member of Parliament that Standing Stillbury had to make a bid to get the factory built in their town. It seemed obvious to him that the company should be offered the ten-acre site at North-End.

The site was part of an industrial estate which contained a small number of other factories, up with which Standing Stillbury put in a self-conscious act of tolerance – this being a place where it was thought more proper to make a living in an office of some kind. It was also near to the North-End Estate which consisted of council houses whose tenants were assumed by most other people of Standing Stillbury to like jolly jobs in factories. It was the only place in the town where there was any real unemployment.

In fact, the chief problem of the North-End Estate concerned jobs.

Most of those who were out of work wanted a job and detested having to collect state hand-outs. They felt the age of universal affluence which was to have followed the technological revolution was passing them by. (They didn't all express this in exactly those words, of course. In some cases their analysis of the economic situation was, with no loss of accuracy, something shorter like 'we're all being f—g ripped off.) The profits of technology were not giving them a good living, with increased leisure time, as predicted in the 1940s. They were simply making the creators and owners of the technology very rich indeed while they struggled to find any kind of work at all. And much of what could be found was menial, low paid, part-time and insecure.

But a minority which had no intention of working felt constantly threatened by the prospect of job offers from the Standing Stillbury Labour Exchange.

The members of this minority were convinced that, as a matter of right, they should be kept by the State in beer and cigarettes and contributions to the local bookie as a reward for their lifetime of contributions to the national insurance system. When pressed about these past contributions, some of them became a little vague and couldn't remember when it was they had last contributed. Some of them were in their early twenties. Despite poor O-level results, if any at all, they had an acute and accurate perception of being on to a good thing.

One resident of the estate had been unable to work for many years as a result of crippling back-trouble. He lived on state invalidity benefit and was the subject of immense sympathy when the Deepshire Planet reported that wicked thieves had deprived him of his only remaining pleasures in life: they had broken into his garden shed one night and taken his gardening tools and his fishing tackle. Yes! I jest not! Gardening tools and fishing tackle. No. He hadn't considered taking up work as a gardener or a fishery bailiff. He had back trouble. It was usually back trouble – or else it was nerves.

But Mr Muffle, as Town Clerk, had to submit a detailed report on the components factory to the Council's Policy Committee. It was clear to the other two that he wanted to outline the advantages and recommend making efforts to persuade the company to come to Standing Stillbury. However, as was perfectly usual, the matter was important enough to be discussed with the Mayor, officially, and the Member of Parliament, unofficially, beforehand.

But the Mayor and the MP had been fumbling for some time around the obviousness of bidding for the factory project. They couldn't quite bring themselves to disagree with the Town Clerk at first – but they couldn't bring themselves to agree either. Their own uncertainty was making them irritable.

'It's not as simple as you think', said the Mayor.

'If we get them here, it's not just the jobs. There's the extra traffic on the roads. The factory will be too big – and what about the rubbish going into the drains?'

'And besides', he went on in a lower tone, 'I've had one or two of the directors at Blank's Bearings getting at me at The Club. They don't want half their workforce going off for better wages when they are only just keeping afloat themselves. Think of that.'

The Club was the local Conservative Club, referred to by unkind detractors from other political parties as the Asil Nadir Memorial Centre. The Mayor had felt indignant when he first heard that jibe. He relished his membership of the Conservative Club as proof of his solid citizenship and, in his case to some extent, it was. But he tried to ignore all that, hoping people would eventually forget who Asil Nadir was. Most already had.

The fact that the mysterious factory was already under discussion outside the council offices was quite normal, despite the confidential nature of the matter. Standing Stillbury was that sort of place. There were networks of inter-family and inter-professional loyalties which could sometimes be traced back for generations. And anyhow, little remained secret for more than 30 minutes after being discussed in a council committee. The Councillors found it essential to impress their families and friends (and, in one or two cases, even friendly journalists), by various subtle means, with the enormity of the information which was entrusted to them. There was, after all, a great danger for those who broke confidentiality late: people might not believe that they had known the secret all along, might think they had only heard it from another councillor and not been in on it from the beginning. That would never do.

Mr Muffle looked up wearily. 'But we've been through all of that, Fred.' (By convention, the Town Clerk was the one borough official who could address the councillors by their first names. For the other officials, it was strictly 'Mr Mayor', 'Councillor', or 'Chairman' for those who held that position on a council committee.) 'If we could get this factory here, it would be worth spending money on a new road into North End – and Blanks would be able to use that as well. And they won't be allowed to put any rubbish down the drains – those days have long gone. And as for the wages at Blanks – I thought you were a Conservative!'

'Of course I am, you know damn well. What do you mean?' replied the Mayor, with puzzlement and irritation.

'Well', said the Town Clerk, his hands meeting at the index fingers an inch or so in front of his chest as he explained his thoughts carefully and slowly, 'Conservatives believe in market forces, don't they?'

He went on without waiting for an answer as the Mayor and the MP looked at each other and then back at him, quizzically. 'That being the case, market forces apply to employers as well as workers. You screw the wages down tightly when jobs are short and people want the work – and the same market forces mean you have to pay more wages to keep people when there are plenty of jobs and they can pick and choose. And if a company can't pay the going rate, and people leave, then maybe they shouldn't be in business any more.'

Mr Muffle spoke with just a little feeling whilst delivering this last sentence. Although a solicitor by profession, as most Town Clerks are, he remembered his own rather more humble origins. His father, a skilled toolmaker and foreman of an entire workshop, had been dismissed from Blanks Bearings when a new managing director, a Brigadier recently de-mobbed from the Deepshire Yeomanry after anonymous war service, had been installed by the influence of friends after the war. Unlike most senior army officers, who make the transition easily enough, this one had never been able to grasp that, in civilian company, people junior to himself would sometimes question his orders and even, on occasion, ask him to explain his logic. This he found trying as he wasn't terribly strong on logic. Within six months he had mentally divided the company into the sycophants and the strong-minded and, by one device or another, got rid of the latter group, including Mr Muffle senior. The whole thing had been presented to the shareholders as an efficiency drive-meaning people were being sacked. The later euphemisms re-structuring, rationalisation, de-layering and right-sizing had not been invented at the time.

This had probably caused the premature death of Mr Muffle's father, nearly ruined Mr Muffle's chance of a university place (saved by the financial kindness of an elderly uncle) and brought great hardship upon his family. The Managing Director left a year later, with a large pay-off from company funds to ensure his silence over disagreements with his former, and now disenchanted, friends on the board. The precise amount of the pay-off had been buried in the annual report under the heading 'administration costs'. The shareholders had known nothing of all this.

But the Mayor and the Member of Parliament looked a bit dumbfounded. The truth was that neither of them was as bright as Mr Muffle ('though they made up for that in forcefulness and political dexterity) and neither of them could quickly find a good answer to what he had said – it was just that they both had a vague sort of feeling that market forces did not exist to push wages UP. That concept was quite extraordinary to them.

Indeed, the Mayor was one of that breed of Conservatives who, oblivious to the contradictions involved, had joined the party as a fierce defender of the rightness of letting market-forces resolve almost all issues. But at one and the same time he was capable of frenzied campaigning against the merest hint of planning permission being granted for a new supermarket within two miles of his own small shop. The latter, he would have reasoned without a trace of embarrassment, would have been part of the remorseless and shameful march of big business trampling over the little man as represented by Fred Meadows. And he would have meant this with complete sincerity.

Of course, his customers would have been no better. They would mostly have thought it perfectly reasonable to rush off to fill their car boots with the cheaper goods from the supermarket. The most shameless would have shopped at the supermarket but come back to Fred Meadows occasionally, when they ran out of money, and found themselves needing the credit which he, but not the supermarkets, allowed. But they would, one and all, with astonishment and dismay, have shed tears about the loss of their beloved and convenient local shop when he closed.

Mr Muffle's reasoning had struck no chord with his two listeners. They looked at him curiously and even wondered if there wasn't a faintly red, or at least lightish pink, tinge to Mr Muffle's politics, left over from his days at university perhaps; a residue of something not yet been completely eroded by a large mortgage and membership of Standing Stillbury Rotary Club. Of course, they would never raise that as an issue since, like all but the most stupid public servants, Mr Muffle kept scrupulously clear of party politics. And the Mayor remembered, a little guiltily, that no Councillor of any party had ever found the Town Clerk unhelpful.

But Jack Fudge had something else to say.

'Bugger the roads and the wages. If you get 500 people working in a car parts factory here, which way do you think they'll all bloody vote? And', he went on, 'the damn Town Forum is already on my back screaming that it would ruin our way of life.'

The Town Forum was an organisation which had no formal powers or elected credentials whatsoever. But, by virtue of an articulate and opinionated membership, it had acquired a great deal of influence in the affairs of Standing Stillbury. In lighter moments it was often referred to as the three-A's – meaning Amateur Aesthetics Association. It consisted for the most part of people who were comfortably off and who had no reason whatsoever to want change and new jobs in The Town. They tended to be members of the professions, teachers, retired civil servants and the like. They were mostly decent, fair-minded sorts who liked to take holidays in Provence or Tuscany and knew a good Claret when it passed under their noses.

The effect of their intervention in town life was not always negative, of course. They had saved many, though not all, of Standing Stillbury's finest buildings from wanton destruction by brash developers. They had even raised money to restore a few of them. Occasionally, they had even found out, God knows how, what heritage-damaging things people were doing inside their own houses and, if a particular house was old enough, had raised a bit of a stink about that.

But they could not really come to terms with new factories, jobs or not. Things like that were, well, not quite Standing Stillbury, were they? For members of the Town Forum, decent folk though they were, the expression 'our way of life', generally meant their particular way of life and not that of the people who lived in places like North End Estate. The 'our' was more selective than collective.

The Town Forum and Jack Fudge had a fairly mutual sense of dislike – something which might be regarded as a point in favour of each of them – but the Forum members mostly voted for him at each successive general election. They did this with an ill-disguised resignation as they didn't want the town represented by someone who was not Conservative and conservative. Some Group members had been on that long-ago committee which had selected Mr Jack Fudge as their prospective candidate. In Standing Stillbury that was as good as giving him the seat. He really had interviewed very well indeed. Their favourable impression had soon worn away but by then it was too late. You didn't change things in Standing Stillbury, least of all the sitting Member of Parliament.

Mr Muffle thought the answers to Jack Fudge's two points were far less obvious than the Member of Parliament seemed to think. People who worked in factories had long-since ceased to be bankable as Labour voters. The way of life of Standing Stillbury, if not that of the Town Forum members specifically, might well be improved by some new jobs. But Mr Muffle knew from long experience that there wasn't any mileage in a deep analysis of the facts with Jack Fudge.

He remembered, with an inward smile, his grandfather telling him, at the age of ten, that you could pin a blue rosette on a donkey in Standing Stillbury and it would be sure to be elected. He looked closely at Mr Fudge but could see no sign of his ears actually getting longer or covered in hair. But Mr Fudge, he realised clearly, must have felt pretty strongly about the matter: his usual tack would have been to grab anything going if only to stop Concrete Hardening getting it. Jack Fudge hated Concrete Hardening and everything it stood for – including its size, its success, its prosperity and its inconveniently intelligent Socialist Member of Parliament, Janus Berkley. But in this case he didn't care if Concrete Hardening got the factory. He simply didn't want it in Standing Stillbury.

These questions hung in the air for a few minutes longer but seemed to drift away without any more words being spoken. Then, the Mayor found one of those magic formulae which experienced politicians use to end any difficult business. 'Look here', he said to the Town Clerk, in a conciliatory way, 'We'll go and have a word with the Chairman of Blank's next week and you can hear exactly what he thinks. Then you can do your report and put it to next month's Policy Committee – a few week's delay won't make any difference. How's that?'

With a resigned expression, the Town Clerk nodded. He put the papers about the factory back into their file and moved on to the impending royal visit when Princess Mary was to open the newly-restored 11th century castle. This was a project which the whole town regarded as something of real importance: Standing Stillbury was nothing if not a town with a castle!

A royal visit raised issues which were very big indeed. Which of the local officials and notables were to be presented to the royal visitor? Could their wives be presented as well? Which of the two local caterers would be given the contract to provide the lunch of transparently thin ham and limp lettuce in the marquee which would be erected in the castle grounds, leaving the other boiling-over like unattended cabbage-water? There was a host of such matters to be settled.

Finding much more productive ground for his political talents, the Mayor cheered up visibly. He took a large sip of his whisky. There were old scores which could be settled in the next hour or so.

Jack Fudge really had no place at what was an entirely civic matter, but he was usually included in business of this kind and, with the unspoken acquiescence of the other two, he stayed for a while. Like the other two, though none of the three would have admitted this, he had been briefed by his wife beforehand and each of the three knew he would have to account for the outcome of the discussions later. That added some sharpness to the ensuing process. Names for presentation to the Princess were put up and accepted or discarded after some discussion in which the Member of Parliament confined himself to the occasional caustic comment, here and there, depending upon Mrs Fudge's view of the candidate.

Eventually, the presentation list was completed for submission to Colonel Haugh, Lord Lieutenant of Deepshire and thus the official representative of the Sovereign in the Shire. Though inclined whenever possible to be helpful, his word would be absolute and final on all matters concerning the royal visit. Those in favour with our triumvirate and their wives, and some others who could not decently be omitted, would be presented to the Princess. Marginal cases who were out of favour, and one known to be currently under investigation for the mis-use of his law firm's clients' account, were excluded. The list might be pruned or even added to by the Lord Lieutenant but the Mayor and the Town Clerk were old hands. They had brought in sufficient names to ensure that any pruning would leave in all those to whom the greatest respect and the biggest favours were owed.

Then they left, the Member of Parliament to drive to London, the Mayor for the Conservative Club and Mr Muffle for home where, he would discover, the fearsome Mrs Muffle intended that he paint the kitchen ceiling before he got any dinner. Mr Muffle's domestic life, with which he put up quite placidly, left him few illusions about the importance of his role in the life of Standing Stillbury.

Chapter 2 – An Opportunity

Whilst all this was going on, it happened that another meeting was taking place in an office at Concrete Hardening, just ten miles away.

This meeting was different from the one just described.

The office was on the tenth and top floor of a tower clad in blue glass which served as the headquarters of Concrete Hardening District Council. It was close to the motorway which probed its way into Deepshire just about this far and a mile or so more towards Standing Stillbury. Long before reaching that town it reverted to the status of a hazardous, single-carriageway, country road although their were plans, it had been rumoured for decades, to improve that section by making it into a dual-carriageway.

The glass tower was well-lit and had wide, double-glazed windows below which could be seen the fruits of twenty years of hard work to persuade people with money (of their own, borrowed or embezzled from pension funds) to invest in the Town. There were several other glass-clad office blocks, separated by carefully groomed areas of landscaping, new roads, bright new shops and two large, modern hotels. Between all these, people and cars moved in all directions. From ten floors up they looked like people and cars observed from ten floors up. In the distance workers were pouring forth from rows of modern, almost gleaming new factory buildings, very few of which were emitting smoke. Most of them, in fact, omitted smoke.

It is worth explaining that one or two of the dirtier industries had managed to set themselves up in Concrete Hardening, having penetrated a rather fierce set of official barriers designed to keep them out. However, they had discovered a method of allaying local anxiety almost totally. They found that, by re-naming their company, painting all their vehicles a certain shade of green and including the word ENVIRONMENTAL in their new title their problems were quickly solved.

Thus Bloggs Industrial Grease Re-cycling became Bloggs Environmental Services and Craggs Used Tyre Processing became Craggs Environmental Processing. The latter still burned the used tyres to extract the metal content but now did it environmentally. It was reminiscent of the way in which, at one time, any country whose name included the words 'people's' and 'democratic' could be guaranteed neither to belong to the people nor to have any electoral system which was capable of removing the ruling elite from power. But there really were very few companies of this type operating in Concrete Hardening.

The Chief Executive of the Council, the equivalent of Mr Muffle at Standing Stillbury, was Henry Morgan. He didn't have Mr Muffle's rather academic air though. He was a bit shorter and stockier, a bit more inclined to get intense about anything in which he was engaged, and his suits were close to a style which might be described as sharp. By background, he was a commercial property surveyor who regarded solicitors like Mr Muffle, whom he knew slightly, as people one employed to tie up the fine details of deals done by people like himself. He was still in his mid-thirties.

Some of the people in the Town didn't like him. This was because he wouldn't join anybody's fund-raising campaign or charity, whatever its purpose. He was always being badgered to get involved with these things but always said no. When they asked him why, he didn't fudge, make excuses or lie politely, as anyone halfway decent would. He just said 'Because I can't stand bloody committees.' People didn't much like that, especially the professional committee dwellers who had nothing much else to do with their lives – but that was Henry Morgan.

He was sitting with the Leader of Concrete Hardening District Council, Ernie Truscott, and the Chairman of the Employment Committee, Brian Fichtl, whose odd name came from Central European parents who had arrived in the area as refugees in 1939. This was not regarded as re-markable. The old and now disappearing traditional industries of the area, mainly metal-bashing, had attracted quite a number of such people who had been assimilated and even welcomed into their new surroundings with much more ease than would have been possible in Standing Stillbury.

Ernie and Brian were both nominally members of the Labour Party – and hated by few enough of its querulous, local members to have gained the elective offices which brought them to Henry Morgan's room. But neither of them had the slightest scruple about supping with the Devil or Conservatives, or any other political faction, if the interests of the town were at stake. Ernie was the owner of a small electrical contracting firm which employed a dozen men, Brian a modern languages teacher. Both could match their Chief Executive for intellect – but seldom felt the need to demonstrate it as they and he all travelled in the same direction most of the time.

Henry Morgan spoke first.

'It seems clear that the Germans are coming to look at Deepshire. You've heard the same rumours as I have and a friend of mine on the Government Investment Panel (known, of course, as GIP) let the name slip when I took him out to dinner in London last night. It's Zugswang of Dusseldorf. They've got to move for some reason and there really could be 500 jobs in it – and as many again with the little fish if we could get them to buy some of their stuff locally.'

All three in this meeting had an air of mild excitement and moved on immediately to the question of how Zugswang might be induced to build their new factory in Concrete Hardening. Curiously, there was no preliminary discussion of whether they wanted them there in the first place. To these people, such a question would have seemed ridiculous.

'I suppose', started Ernie, 'that we might fiddle some Assisted Area cash to get them settled in, and sell them a slice of the Riverside Campus for as low a price as we can furtle past the District Valuer.'

'We'll need all of that and more', mused the Chief Executive. 'Every other bloody place with a vacant factory site will be after them, as usual, and they apparently need at least eight acres with the planning permission sorted out quickly when they take a decision. I've got, off the record of course, an outline of the building shape and site layout they want. It'd make a nice big hole in our unemployment if we could swing this one.'

Brian Fichtl casually picked up the Chief Executive's internal telephone and asked the Chief Planner Mr Clamp if he could join them. For an elected member to have summoned a chief officer in this way, and on the Chief Executive's telephone to boot, would have been regarded as an unthinkable breach of manners at Standing Stillbury. In Concrete Hardening, the councillor's action was unremarkable and went quite unremarked.

It was 6.30 pm but no surprise to find Mr Clamp still in the building.

He arrived in a minute or so, having guessed the reason for the call. He was a serious sort, rapidly balding and given to wearing yesterday's suits, a Yorkshireman who had worked for four other local councils during a long career. On arriving at Concrete Hardening he had been quite pleased (the farthest Mr Clamp normally went in adjectives about his own feelings) to discover something he had been seeking for years. It was a place where people paid him to plan for things to happen. All his previous councils had employed planners to stop things happening. Mr Clamp's unusual preference, as planners went, had been observed by his present employers with increasing pleasure and, to his slight embarrassment, they had become prone to boasting about him to visiting delegations from other Councils, good naturedly exhibiting him as an example of a rare and valuable species – which, in a sense he was.

The fact was that Mr Clamp understood the rules and regulations of planning as well as the next planner – and better than most. But whenever they seemed likely to thwart some opportunity to improve the lot of Concrete Hardening, he made it his personal job to find a way around the problem.

'Ah', said Brian Fichtl, 'We wanted a word about Riverside Campus. We've got a prospect from abroad. It needs eight acres or so. Henry's wangled an outline of the site and building requirements – d'you think it could be sorted quickly if we got them interested?'

Mr Clamp pulled up a chair and one of the others poured him a cup of coffee. 'Yes', he replied after a moment, 'If you can let me have the bones of the project I could get things moving. Riverside's already got general consent for industry, so my people could virtually draft the application for this specific factory and have it ready for the company to sign and then stick it in front of the Committee. Of course, we've agreed to talk to the locals with each new factory plan for Riverside – but I could do that and you'd just need to agree to call a special meeting of the Planning Committee meeting very quickly if the normal date didn't fit the timescale.'

'I assume', he went on gently, though in a heavy Yorkshire accent, 'that this is Zugswang – the word is going around in one or two circles!'

The others chuckled. Mr Clamp, like Henry Morgan, had acquired some good contacts during his career. Both men understood the value of good contacts and cultivated them with the utmost care, like peas in dry soil.

'Right', replied Ernie Truscott with a grin, 'and let me know if those silly sods in Technical Services try to slow this one up with ten-foot concrete foundations or whatever this month's new buggeration factor is!'

The others snorted and nodded their heads in agreement with this sentiment.

But the comment was really unnecessary. Some years before, Concrete Hardening had lost the chance of some hundreds of jobs when a zealous structural engineer, one of the Council's own men, had driven a French company to distraction with his excessive, heavily over-calculated demands for foundations, load-bearing beams, supporting walls and a clutter of similar things. The French had put up with so much and then abruptly gone away to build their factory elsewhere.

This lesson was burned into the corporate soul of Concrete Hardening District Council. Its less visionary minor officials had been warned, strictly off the record, that jobs came first, bureaucratic rules (and ESPECIALLY bureau-

cratic rules from the EEC) a long way second. Industry was
to be welcomed.

Council staff quite unconcerned with industrial development might even be hauled out of their routine jobs to help
things along, especially if they happened to speak the
language of any foreign company with which the Council
was dealing. Some of the older, grandee-style chief officers,
people who came into the office less during the shooting
season and were always missing during Ascot week, had
been outraged by this method of working, resisting fiercely
the idea that THEIR Mr Smith or Mr Jones could be called
upon by another department in its hour of need. By the time
of these events such departmental dinosaurs had either
been converted or levered out of the Council's employment
to be replaced by people who could think sideways.

By this time, Henry Morgan had already tracked down
the Chairman of the Council's Planning Committee at his
house and, by telephone, gained his agreement in principle
to a meeting at very short notice if one were needed. One
or two of the shorter-sighted councillors might grumble at
the haste of the proceedings. One or two of the more self-
important would complain at being summoned without
more deference to their work commitments. But both main
political parties at Concrete Hardening District Council,
whilst quarrelling in the way of political parties, were united
in the matter of factories with jobs. They both saw new jobs
as the key to almost everything else they wanted to achieve
for the Town. Any dissidents would be suppressed and only
those councillors glowing with approval would be allowed
anywhere near a delegation from the Zugswang Company,
if one could be persuaded to come.

This fact, incidentally, led inexorably to an interesting
conclusion. It meant that most of Concrete Hardening's
councillors, whatever their political party, were instinctively
radical and rather adventurous in outlook. Most of Standing
Stillbury's, Tory, Socialist or Liberal, were instinctively
conservative with a small 'c'. In each case, it was the nature
of the town, at least as much as the party, which gave it's
genetic imprint to the political outlook of the councillors.

Mr Clamp had been scribbling details whilst the others

were talking. He finished his coffee and excused himself from the meeting so as to start thinking his way through the planning application, for a company which didn't yet know it was making one, that very evening.

The two councillors remained with the Chief Executive for a while to talk about another problem which loomed as large in the politics of Concrete Hardening as the impending royal visit did in Standing Stillbury. They didn't have an impending royal visit to worry about. Their problem was the gypsy site.

All local councils were supposed to have gypsy sites. These were sites where any group of people other than actual gypsies could park their caravans for a small or large number of days as the fancy took them. They consisted, in fact, of a mixture of Irish scrap dealers, English scrap dealers (both types of dealer displaying a singular lack of written records), miscellaneous un-washed rogues and the socially disaffected. The socially disaffected were people who felt they didn't belong in society and therefore had no liability for either general taxation or the specific road tax required to be paid in respect of their vehicles. They formed the one single class of motorist seldom troubled by the police in this respect or any other. And despite their self-assumed non-liability for anything, they all knew exactly how to collect substantial sums of our money which a generous and forgiving government seemed happy to re-distribute in their direction, in whatever town with a social security office they happened to be on Tuesdays. It was then cheerfully spent on cans of high-gravity premium lager whose powers of alcoholic transmutation would bring on deep and brooding philosophical discussions on just why and how they had come to have no part in society. Sometimes, though not often it must be admitted, these discussions would become so deep and brooding as to end in a violent punch-up.

These people exposed a little appreciated advantage of unpopular indirect taxes such as VAT and the excise duties levied on petrol, tobacco and alcohol. They might not cough up any income tax, but since they simply couldn't avoid paying indirect taxes in the course of buying what they and their children didn't steal, the Exchequer did at least extract a small contribution from them.

The theory of gypsy sites was that their availability would dissuade the travellers from turning up at the boundary of someone's private land in the early hours of the morning, smashing expensive gates or barriers, moving in with any number of vans and sitting tight until the exact day before a court-order to get them off was due to be enforced. Since this process usually took about two weeks they had quite a nice system going. And no-one had ever thought of seizing one of the vans against payment for the repairs to the gate and clearance of the disgusting mess usually left on the site. If they had, the police would very likely have reacted quite firmly. THAT, of course, would have been QUITE against the law.

The liberal, small 'l', consciences of Concrete Hardening's left-leaning professional classes and opinion-formers were, however, united in their view that the travellers were really good people whose freedom to roam should be facilitated by the provision of a decent site in this and every other district throughout the land. But there was a curious law of municipal physics which seemed to impede every attempt by Concrete Hardening Council to establish a site.

The problem was this. By the very nature of a gypsy site, it had to be somewhere, in an actual place. You couldn't simply create one as a concept. (Or, in more usual council parlance for something that was really nothing, 'an initiative'.) It needed to have existence, physically as well as metaphysically, on a piece of ground. Once created, caravans had to be allowed on to it and, with the caravans, their owners and their families. And strangely, the most liberal consciences became desperately agitated when any idea of this happening near their house was mooted.

It wasn't, of course, that the travellers were inclined to thieving, leaving heaps of stinking and unsightly rubbish about, defecating in the open, generally wrecking property values or keeping dogs which all seemed to have unusually large sexual organs and looked as if they didn't pay income tax either. Oh no! Dear me no! The travellers were such lovely people, free spirits and all that, were they not? That wasn't the problem at all.

It was, you understand, simply that the suggested site was always totally UNSUITABLE – in the opinion of everyone living within about a mile that is. It might have been earmarked for something else in the town development plan, access from the nearest road might be too dangerous, it might be too far from schools and shops or, alternatively, it might be too near to them.

Even worse, the land might, suddenly, be found to be supporting a large population of wild birds and lepidoptera (it almost always was) and have to be declared, as an emergency measure, a site of special scientific interest. In that event, bearded men of earnest demeanour could always be found to support the hypothesis in grave tones, in interviews given to Radio Deepshire. Even over the radio, you could tell they had a beard. 'The population of speckled wood butterflies would be in great danger and as for the lesser spotted woodpeckers . . . . . .' You know the sort of thing. In the future, no doubt, this concern will extend even to exotic and rare forms of bacteria found to be living in the soil itself, on the very site under discussion and no-where else in the World.

But if all these failed, there was one super new idea which had become the height of fashion amongst the NIMBY, NODAM and 'put-it-somewhere-else' classes: 'The ground was contaminated by past industrial activity.'

The technique was so simple. You quickly got an expert in to examine some soil from the site. In this case he would be bald-headed and wearing a white coat. He would find minute traces of lead or cadmium or some other noxious metal. He would deliver his verdict whilst holding a testtube of some un-defined murky liquid, the content of which would not be referred to directly. The matter would be leaked (not literally of course) to the Deepshire Planet and reported sensationally in sinking-of-the-Titanic sized headlines. 'LAND POISONED!' And another gypsy site would be lost.

No-one ever explained that most of Concrete Hardening was built on ground containing traces of a dirty industrial past, or, indeed, how the gypsies were supposed to be harmed by parking their vans on such land legally for a couple of weeks in the year when they had been doing it for years illegally. (Local children would have played unharmed in the lethal soil for decades.)

The inconsistency of the claims about a delicately balanced ecology, the bird life and lepidoptera, when set against the deadly poisons in the land, would be quite overlooked. It was enough that, to the intense relief of all nearby, the site had been found to be unsuitable. Within a few years, new houses would have been built on it and the contamination never referred to again – least of all in the estate agents' brochures.

So the provision of a gypsy site turned into an endless, years-long game of pass the parcel. Whole generations of elected councillors demonstrated their political virility by supporting the principle wholeheartedly but keeping the actuality off their own little patch at any cost. Each was terrified that the music might stop when a site in his ward was under discussion and that he might be left holding a parcel he desperately didn't want to win.

And the sinister under-current of this debate was that the majority party on the Council might one day foist a gypsy site onto an ungrateful ward which had voted a Conservative into office, as punishment for its foolishness and poor judgment. At any event, the suggestion of putting one in a Conservative-held ward immediately evinced this allegation which was, of course, incapable of proof either way. Lower Middle Sniffley was particularly quick to brand any new idea affecting itself as Labour revenge for electing Conservative councillors for the wards which lay in that most reactionary part of Concrete Hardening.

So the discussion of the gypsy site by Roger Morgan and the two councillors was doomed to be much less productive than anything they had said about Zugswang Components of Dusseldorf.

'Look', said Roger, without any of the conviction and enthusiasm with which he had approached the previous topic of discussion, 'We really have to make some sort of progress on this. Don't you think Archie Gibbons can convince people in his ward that the Greenlea site is possible. It's at least 200 yards from all but two houses and we could even buy-out the owners if they want? We can plant bloody trees around the whole place so it looks like a patch of woodland from outside.'

Archie Gibbons was the Councillor for Greenlea. He was Labour, sound, old-fashioned, un-extreme and a genuine democrat. He was the sort of socialist who shuddered inwardly at being made to refer to chairmen of committees as 'chairs' and, for that matter, at any other form of prescribed political correctness. He tended to shudder even more at the sort of people who did the prescribing.

In fact, he was in bad odour with some of his younger comrades that evening. Earlier in the day, Concrete Hardening's Library Committee had considered with great seriousness a proposal to burn the existing stock of children's books by Captain W E Johns (the author of Biggles) and by Frank Richards (who created Billy Bunter) on the grounds that both could be considered racist and, in the case of the latter, fatist as well! (Noddy books had already been put to the flames as dwarfist and earist)

The real truth was that both writers represented a particular strand of English life which some of the comrades disliked intensely. But Archie Gibbons had managed to get half the committee laughing at the idea by asking whether Ernest Hemingway and Joseph Conrad were to be treated similarly for their occasional use of long obsolete terms to describe black people. Since even the comrades classed the latter two writers as 'serious', and they were foreign-born and thus very much more important than English writers, this had put them in a bit of a quandary. So the book burning decision had been deferred which meant it opening up to debate in the local newspapers and even more laughter directed at the aspiring burners. The comrades didn't like being laughed at for their earnest endeavours to create lightness and joy throughout the World and Archie would pay for the fact sooner or later.

But Brian Fichtl looked glum. 'I'm sorry, Henry. I've tried everything on the old sod (this last said with much more affection than malice) and he won't budge. Say's he'll have the site in Greenlea over his dead body and that if we arrange for that (this said with a rueful grin) we'll lose the ward next May. The Tories are using it locally to screw us and Archie told me to fuck off!' (The impact of such an unfortunate remark, made by one Labour councillor to another in Concrete Hardening, should not be rated too heavily – it was little more than a comradely rejection of a given proposition and certainly accepted as such by Councillor Fichtl.)

'Bugger', was the Chief Executive's reply, 'that was our last real hope for a while. You know this has been going on for about twenty years now – I read back through the file a few days ago. Have you any idea where it was first suggested the site might be, the very first time the Council looked at it?'

'No', chorussed the other two, neither of whom had been councillors for that long.

'Greenlea!', said Henry Morgan – and since then we've considered twenty-two others, and here we are back again.'

'We'd better leave it for now', he went on, 'Let's try and make something happen with Zugswang instead.'

The councillors agreed. They left to start smoothing the path of the German factory amongst their party colleagues at the Labour Club.

Henry Morgan remained in his office and during the following hour he made a number of telephone calls, some in German which he spoke with reasonable fluency. Concrete Hardening maintained a small office in Germany and the two members of staff who worked there – at any time of day or night necessary – were asked to gather all the available information about Zugswang Components, quickly.

The Chief Executive's penultimate call established that a delegation from Zugswang would be looking at sites in the UK within ten days and that they could probably be persuaded to include Concrete Hardening in their tour.

The final call was to a junior minister in the Industry Department who was persuaded to alter his diary and bring forward a planned visit so as to coincide with that of the delegation from Germany. This might have been regarded as curious. Despite Concrete Hardening's unyielding

Labour politics, Conservative Ministers were easily persuaded to visit it. (They were seldom seen in Standing
Stillbury.) The fact was that the Government rather liked a
place where things happened – and a certain generosity
with grant funding had frequently allowed them to share
with local Labour councillors the political credit for some
new development in a way which neither side begrudged
the other. Even the more traditional Deepshire land-owning
squires, whilst paying lip service to Standing Stillbury,
actually put their money into Concrete Hardening and used
their clout with this or that Government Department if the
Town occasionally needed their help.

In this particular case, the Junior Minister was Warren
Clews-Lessly who, despite some odd personal quirks,
controlled a good deal of grant money and had a clear
understanding about job-creation. With a silver-spooned
aristocratic background, he secretly found a few beers with
boisterous, pushy Labour Councillors a shade more to his
liking than vinegar-dry sherry with some of the blue-rinsed
Little Englander matrons he often found trying to boss him
around in his own political circles out in the shires.

Chapter 3 – A Visit

Fred Meadows had been as good as his word. At the end of the meeting in the Mayor's Parlour, he had met the Chairman of Blank's Bearings at the Conservative Club and, with some difficulty, arranged a visit for himself and Mr Muffle. The Mayor was to take the Town Clerk to be persuaded that Standing Stillbury didn't want a new factory.

The Chairman, Sir Blathwell Scam, was even more portly and red-faced than the Mayor. He was not accustomed to persuading people. He was accustomed to telling them. That had accounted for the Mayor's difficulty in persuading him of the need for the meeting. Over many years at Blank's Bearings Sir Blathwell's ability to discuss company matters rationally had gradually reduced to the point at which few of his fellow board-members and senior executives felt able to question him about anything. Attempts to do so led to a sharp increase in blood-pressure manifested by histrionics, splenetic rage, and an intensification of the facial reddening. Most of the people around Sir Blathwell preferred a quieter life. Without being conscious of the fact he had, in recent years, only appointed senior staff calculated to like a quieter life. In his own way, he was repeating the damaging cycle of talent-stripping which had cost Mr Muffle's father his job at the Company many years before.

Sir Blathwell's Knighthood had come a few years earlier. The events were quite un-connected, of course, but there had been a long period of financial contributions by Blank's Bearings to Conservative Party funds. The shareholders had never been consulted about the contributions which had not been identifiable in the annual reports. They were reduced sharply after the Knighthood was bestowed upon a grateful Chairman and his even more grateful wife who revelled conspicuously in the title Lady Scam.

Sir Blathwell planned to retire in another year or so. He would enforce a contract of employment which promised a golden handshake which, by this time of decline, would amount to about half the company's cash assets. There would also be a very large pension which would put a severe strain on the pension fund and cause the retired manual employees to be given below-inflation increases for some years ahead. They would never be told the reason or think to connect Sir Blathwell's retirement with the diminishing values of their own incomes.

The rest of the Board of Blank's Bearings would approve Sir Blathwell's personal financial plans on the nod, without any hint of dissent. Several of them were chairmen or board members of other ageing companies and would want the favour returned by Sir Blathwell and people like him at future board meetings of their own. They would all say what a splendid job he had done during the most difficult trading conditions any of them could remember and how, if you wanted the best people, you had to pay the market rate. The market rate for the best people was something they all had a vested interest in pushing up at around four times the rate of inflation and six times the rate permitted to the employees.

This cosy, quite un-written and informal team-spirit amongst networks of company board members worked splendidly for them all. Individual shareholders tended to fret from time to time but their protests were always squashed by the massed voting power of large share-owning institutions whose board members, as you might guess, also had a strong interest in maintaining the upward spiral of boardroom remuneration – an important-sounding word much preferred to the more prosaic pay.

And there was a hidden beauty to this arrangement. Even if a chairman or managing director was judged to be so disastrous a failure that his removal was quite un-avoidable, he would always prove to have a contract which provided for an enormous pay-off, even in that sad event. A man needed just one top-level appointment with a certain sort of company to have secured his future. A company executive might devote his whole career to manoeuvring through the game to land on a golden square. Once attained, inadequacy, failure and enforced departure, even after just a few months, would leave him with the equivalent of a very large win on the football pools. He had won the gin and tonic jackpot, the boardroom bonanza, and would never need to work again, his family insulated from financial worry – perhaps for generations if the cash were invested wisely and taxation and death duties carefully evaded.

In due course, Sir Blathwell planned to join some of the long-spent forces from other companies on the boards of various government initiatives designed to encourage this or that aspect of other people's business affairs. These organisations were, by and large, full of people who were past doing very much themselves – but who loved to tell others how to do them. Sometimes they even started taking on full time employees to help to tell people how to do things – often smartly-dressed women who wandered from room to room carrying sheaves of paper, complaining to each other on what an aaaw-ful week it was. No-one ever saw these jobs advertised or was able to fathom where the women had come from.

The retired Sir Blathwells and their kind often astonished themselves by the new clarity of vision they developed when it was other people's money which was being risked in a new venture of some kind.

Those who hadn't already got there, often found themselves in the honours list after a few years of such self-sacrifice, though adamant, if asked, that the possibility of a CBE or OBE had never entered their heads.

Eventually, there would be so many advice and training agencies, staffed by people who couldn't actually make a living doing anything very much themselves, that sharp competition would develop to track down the dwindling number of people to whom advice on running a business could actually be offered. There would be fierce clashes with marauding gangs of BS 5750 consultants who were targeting the same scarce prey.

But right now, Sir Blathwell Scam was still the Chairman of Blank's Bearings – and he didn't want Zugswang

Components of Dusseldorf building a new factory in Standing Stillbury. His own company's pay rates for shop-floor workers were very low indeed and he was determined there would be no defections to a rival employer with a consequent creeping-up of wages as he sought to replace them. With another British company of similar ilk it might have been possible to reach an unspoken understanding about this. But with bloody Germans, he had reflected, there would be no hope. They would pay less than the sterling equivalent of their rates in Dusseldorf – but that would still be too much for Blanks to match.

So, he had growled and grumbled but agreed to the Mayor's suggested meeting and resolved to feign politeness to Mr Muffle. He had never met Mr Muffle before, but concluded that anyone wanting new jobs in the town must be some sort of upstart. A day was set for the meeting. Mr Muffle would travel with the Mayor in the official Standing Stillbury car, complete with its flag bearing the town's historic coat of arms.

On the day, at 9.00 am prompt, the Mayor and the Town Clerk met on the steps of the Town Hall. Their dark suits, newly pressed, and their grooming, marked them out from most of the passers-by, who shuffled to their jobs in shops and offices, clad in anoraks with fur-edged hoods or cheap mackintoshes, carefully avoiding the dog-droppings which punctuated – they were often comma-shaped – the grammatical flow of the town's pavements.

The chauffeur, Mr Horrocks, awaited them at the rear, nearside door of an ageing, though genteel, Daimler Sovereign which, with some good natured assistance from Mr Mondelski, had received a deal more care than he that morning. Whilst the black bodywork of the car gleamed, Mr Horrocks didn't. He wore a suit of some brown, man-made fibre that wasn't quite up to its task. His face had the pleasant but slightly blurred look of someone who had spent a long time in the bar of the Bear Hotel the previous evening. His baldness was concealed by a peaked hat, of the same brown as his suit, which bore the cockade of the Corps of Chauffeurs.

Mr Horrocks hated that peaked hat. Neither the present

Mayor nor he had dreamed it up. It had been the idea of Miss Peeves who set great store by refinements of this kind. A few years earlier she had convinced the Mayor of that time, a man of great personal conceit, of the cleverness of the idea – and that had been an end to the matter. Any subsequent neglect of the hat brought forth an immediate reprimand from Miss Peeves whose real power, in the event of any defiance, was notoriously difficult to judge. Mr Muffle was known to indulge her, as part of the unwritten contract which delivered fierce loyalty to him in return. No-one had yet gambled on how far that indulgence might stretch. Besides, there would surely be a better reason than the hat to put it to the test one day.

The two-mile journey to Blank's Bearings at North End took 25 minutes through choked streets designed, if they had been designed at all, for the ox-carts of eight or nine hundred years before. They passed under the station bridge, a curious relic from the previous century. This monument to Victorian enterprise had left one end of Standing Stillbury Railway Station built over some of the town roads, supported by heavy brick arches, now heavily scored by the roofs of lorries whose cowboy-drivers had ignored the warnings of low clearance. The other end projected right across the River Septon, where a metal bridge was supported by massive cast-iron columns, around which the river swirled impotently at Summer-low or Winter flood alike. Shoals of barbel, heads firmly against the current, muscled their way into the swirls which delivered food to them from the quieter reaches upriver.

The whole area around the station attracted shoals of taxi-drivers – both of the black cab and the private hire variety. The two types of vehicle were driven, as Mr Muffle had observed, quite differently. It was summed-up by the clothes worn by the drivers. Those in the black cabs had dark, sober jackets of shiny, past-its-best material and some even wore ties. They had bored, fed-up expressions come Winter or Summer but always took the most direct route to their destinations. The others were more cheerful. They wore stetson hats and check shirts. When they came back from delivering a fare, they hitched their taxis by a piece of rope to a wooden rail running along the pavement outside the Station – as if they might run off whilst their owners visited the station buffet. From time to time their driving technique caused mild reproaches to be uttered by the citizens of the Borough.

Just beyond the town part of the railway bridge lay the postal sorting office for all of Deepshire and many of the surrounding counties. The town's businesses had the privilege of posting late mail at the sorting office, through one of two adjoining letter-boxes in the wall, marked 'ordinary mail' and 'franked mail'. Mr Muffle, who had a small streak of quizzicality, remembered once peeping through the letter boxes and observing that all the mail put into either fell down stainless-steel chutes which converged and spilled the letters into the same canvas-lined wicker basket.

The first contact any visitor made with Blank's Bearings was the gatehouse, a square brick-built hut outside of which was a raising-barrier mechanism and inside of which sat two hard-faced, uniformed security men reading newspapers.

As the mayoral car pulled up before the barrier, there was no immediate reaction. After a few seconds, one of the guards glanced up from his paper, The Daily Sport, grimaced, folded it slowly and carefully and then casually beckoned Mr Horrocks to approach the hut. At first the gesture was misunderstood, Mr Horrocks having found that, however other people might be treated, security men usually reacted to the Mayor's flag-decked car with a modicum of respect. So he cheerfully waved back, expecting the barrier to be raised.

It wasn't. The guard, clearly annoyed, gestured more vigorously and mouthed the words 'Over here, chum', through the hut window. The word 'chum' was not used to convey any sense of amity. Bemused, Mr Horrocks left the car and approached the hut. The window was opened with a sideways sliding motion, a book shoved towards him, accompanied by the words 'Sign here.', the face from which the words had emerged now looking down again at the cover of the folded newspaper.

His eyes momentarily raising towards Heaven, Mr Horrocks signed. He also filled in his time of arrival, the name of the person being visited, the registration number of the Mayoral car and wrote 'Standing Stillbury Borough Council' in the column headed 'name of company'.

These details were briefly examined and, after some calculated and insolent deliberation, one guard strolled slowly to raise the barrier-arm whilst the other continued to read. The gate-house at Blanks had always been run like this. No-one had ever thought to question its necessity or to relate its operation in any way to the Company's need to be polite to potential customers. There were six guards who worked in pairs on eight-hourly shifts. They reported to the Assistant Head of Security with whom they had last had any face-to-face contact three months before.

The Security Section of Management, and its six guards, had a nil score in detecting the theft of metal parts, some specially customised by the thieves on the Company's own machines, which was practised extensively within the works. They simply didn't dare approach internal security with the suspicious rigour imposed upon visitors. 'The men', and more particularly their union, wouldn't have stood for it. The actual detection of a theft would have been regarded personal victimisation as well as an insult to the dignity of the workers and a good reason for an immediate and damaging walk-out. The Company needed a managing director who would shake the place up and let the walk-out happen – if only to see which side would lose its nerve first. But that wasn't in the immediate plans of Blank's Bearings.

The five separate factory buildings were not a good advertisement for the Town. They were of varied ages, some going back as far as the 1870s. All were patched and mended with assorted corrugations and panels which no-one had ever bothered to have painted in matching colours. Despite the makeshift repairs, the roof of each building leaked here and there and during bad winters the men inside shivered a good deal.

But there was work going on. It had been going on for a good two hours by the time they arrived. The banging, clanging, buzzing, roaring, grinding and screeching of ancient machines testified to production taking place, though of what exactly, neither the Mayor nor Mr Muffle were sure. Had the visitors looked inside, they would have seen a confusion of men in grimy overalls, oil-stained floors and heaps of half-swept metal trimmings and other assorted rubbish. The rubbish lay between enormous presses, cutting machines, die-stampers and drop forges – many bearing dates and the names of long-extinct Victorian machine manufacturers from places like Tipton and Dewsbury. And these days not every machine was in gainful employment. Some just sat, with a forlorn and redundant air about them, rust slowly building up on once bright cutting edges.

Here and there were piles of metal castings, rusting and un-moved for years, their purpose long forgotten, the liklihood of their being removed in a general tidy-up, small. There was no new machinery at all.

But they were not going to the factory buildings. Mr Horrocks drove past them by a good hundred yards to a large office block, brick-built and with the aluminium window frames of the 1950s, at which the important people of Blank's Bearings arrived in leisurely fashion between nine and ten o'clock each weekday morning. Over the door, the words 'Blank's Bearings Ltd' appeared in twelve-inch high white-painted metal letters. But the 'B' had fallen off 'Bearings' six months before. Such was the convoluted bureaucracy of the place that it wouldn't be replaced for another six months at least. No-one was allowed simply to go and get a replacement. The systems of management and financial control imposed by past decades of managers and financial controllers had extinguished the tiniest remaining sparks of initiative. Everything, however small, had to go through the company system, with forms, approvals and specified rubber stampings needed at every management checkpoint along the way. All this was supposed to prevent wasted expenditure. But it was helping to kill the company. The staff costs of administering the systems at Blank's were far in excess of the savings they were achieving. No one had ever considered this possibility and done anything about it.

Of course, those who wore smart suits and signed things at different points in the system had a strong interest in keeping things as they were. In the meantime, with the large, white 'B' still missing, those who didn't know better might have assumed that the company made jewellery of some sort.

In fact, of the total workforce at Blank's, some 2,000 people, around a quarter, five hundred or so, worked in the office block producing nothing the company could sell. There were secretaries, clerks, salesmen, buyers, middle managers, book-keepers, auditors, senior managers, heads of this, heads of that, personal assistants to some of those listed and directors and board members. They all felt a certain contempt for people who worked at the Town Hall which, they were sure, was over-staffed and bureaucratic compared with the thrusting and competitive private sector in which they worked.

Despite some considerable differences in status and salary amongst this large group of people they all, to their own immense relief, shared the common ground of working in the offices, or, put another way, not working in the factories. This was a desperately important matter to most of them. They felt their whole standing in the Town, and in the neighbourhoods in which they lived, depended upon not being seen to make anything useful. Very few of them, and that included their Chairman, had ever spent much time in the factory buildings. The senior people preferred to deal with what happened in the factory buildings as a sort of abstraction, something to be worked out on paper and communicated by memoranda to the few people whose jobs occasionally forced them out of the offices to explain what products the men were required to produce next.

But the differences between the office dwellers were important as well. To some extent, the variations in status could be measured by salaries or by which of the three different dining rooms an office employee was entitled to use: that reserved for the board members' representing the pinnacle of corporate dining, with silver cutlery (or silver-plated at any rate), delicate china and waitress service. The dining rooms for middle-management and clerical staff were very, very carefully graded downwards from that.

The factory workers, it might be mentioned, were fed well away from the offices in a depressing canteen building appended to one of the sheds in which they worked. Loudly

spoken, white coated ladies of enormous girth and raucous-
ness greeted them across a stainless steel counter where
their plates were piled with chips, more chips and stodgy
meat pies of one kind or another. Such vegetables as were
provided were always boiled to near-anonymity. Thick
gravy was poured across everything, including the chips.
All the touchable surfaces in the works canteen were
covered with a thin film of air-borne grease.

But these things were less significant than the blue
enamel plaques, with white lettering, by the reserved
parking spaces.

Each of these plaques, there were exactly forty of them,
was fixed, by four round-headed brass screws, to a low brick
wall which ran along the front of the offices, one every
seven feet or so, bearing the name and the precise title of the
person for whom the space was reserved.

The plaques carried huge significance at Blank's Bearings. The death or retirement of the possessor of one always
started a frenzy of jockeying and lobbying by potential
claimants throughout the building. The office became like
a safe parliamentary seat when the sitting member had died
or retired in disgrace. It was neither explained nor understood precisely who took the final decision to re-allocate a
parking space, or exactly when the decision was taken – but
the word would emerge from the top floor eventually.
Then, the lucky recipient would have a new plaque ordered
from a small company a few hundred yards away which
struggled along from year to year, scraping a living from
companies like Blank's Bearings, using equipment as old
and outdated as theirs. When the new plaque arrived, the
favoured employee would proudly supervise its fixing to the
wall in the sure knowledge that his career had taken an
upward turn. It has to be said 'his' career. No blue plaque
had ever, up to the time of writing, been allocated to a
woman employee. No woman had ever risen above the
level of senior secretary at Blank's Bearings.

Those staff without the coveted reserved spaces had to
make do with the office general parking area. Although
separated from it by a wire mesh fence, this ran alarmingly
close to the factory parking area, packed with Ladas, Skodas

and a variety of ageing British cars which were generally maintained by their owners in the front gardens of their council houses at the weekends. They sometimes became so good at this work that other people's cars would appear for repairs as well, providing a nice, but unsightly, little sideline, un-detected by the Inland Revenue. Sometimes a strange vehicle would appear and remain for weeks, one or two wheels removed, their places taken by small stacks of bricks. The more sensitive neighbours would complain bitterly to the Council. After a few weeks a housing inspector would arrive, usually to find that the offending vehicle had, miraculously, been removed the day before. Sometimes, though, he would be forced into retreat before a torrent of abuse and expletives and claims that the vehicle was owned by the tenant. Whether owned by the tenant or not, the common factor between the two categories of vehicle under repair was a total absence of road tax discs.

The staff at Blank's lived in dread of being thought by outside observers to park with the factory workers or, even worse, of having their cars broken into or stolen by them. It never actually happened – but they all assumed it might.

Those without them would have given half their salaries for the status the blue plaques conferred. The news of a new plaque-allocation would spread like an oil-slick across the surface of the Company, its staff and their wives, causing anger or malicious glee, depending upon the place of the hearer in the complex network of relationships in the offices. There would be angry, furtive discussions in hidden corners. The recipient of a plaque was always, in the view of some, a shameless, brainless crawler who had slimily ingratiated himself with the management. Others would praise the decision to allocate the plaque whilst calculating how the new status of their colleague might be turned to personal advantage.

No-one ever complained directly to a senior manager about this process or anything else at Blank's. It just wasn't that sort of place. Events which caused resentment or dismay to members of staff were simply muttered about endlessly, in the corridors or in the offices, amongst people who were more or less employed at the same level. This cost the Company a huge amount of wasted time. But the idea of going and thrashing a problem out with a senior manager would have astonished both sides and been quite unthinkable.

Of course, there was no parking for visitors. Sales representatives, job interviewees and even people who might have been able to place large orders for the company's products, all had to take their chance at the far end of the general staff area. The parking spaces with the blue plaques, naturally closest to the office entrance, were guarded fiercely at further cost in staff time. Any visitor who failed to realise this and parked in a vacant space would be seen from several different office windows and a security man sent to remove him before he had even left his vehicle. Sometimes the manner of the removal was so offensive that the visitor got back into his car and left, the purpose of his visit never being explained and, worse, not even speculated about. The crucial thing was that he had been kept out of the reserved parking space.

These holy places were all occupied by company cars which, curiously, got bigger and less British as the company profits got lower and closer to an annual loss. This was deemed necessary. It wasn't, you will understand, for the privilege of the individuals. It was so that the company cars would give the right impression of prosperity to visitors from other archaic companies, equally doomed, who themselves arrived in quite splendid cars for exactly the same reason.

However, the imposing livery of the Mayoral car told Mr Horrocks, with some certainty, that he might be able to get away with drawing up to the foot of the office steps, which he did.

As he did so, Sir Blathwell's Secretary, Miss Prewitt, a figure strangely like that of Miss Peeves at the Town Hall, hurried down the steps looking flustered. Sir Blathwell was late arriving for the meeting. Miss Prewitt began to explain, without real conviction, that he had been delayed in heavy traffic when a large, chauffeur-driven Mercedes saloon, in metallic silvery-grey, pulled up behind the Mayoral car.

A casually dressed Sir Blathwell struggled out before his

driver could get around the vehicle to open his door. He
wore a flat tweed cap, a jacket of similar material, plus-fours
and brown leather brogue shoes.

'Sorry about that', said Sir Blathwell, in a sort of grunt
which suggested he wasn't. 'Got half way to the golf course
when I suddenly remembered I should have been here.
Damned inconvenient. Had to stand up my partner.'

'Mm', said the Mayor, whose standing in the Town
Clerk's eyes was hardly to be improved by this admission.

'Anyhow, come in, come in,' went on Sir Blathwell, leading them up the steps to the door through which Miss
Prewitt had quickly retreated, muttering, when his appearance and explanation spoiled her traffic story.

As they disappeared, Mr Horrocks was invited to follow
Sir Blathwell's driver in another direction. The two of them
went to a small portacabin-type building in which the other
company drivers congregated when not at the wheel. They
were nominally available for general handyman duties
during these periods but spent most of the time drinking tea,
playing darts and reading newspapers and lurid magazines
which featured large-bosomed women, undressed and in
strange poses. Any call upon their time would be measured
carefully against the position in the company of the caller.
If he was too important to be ignored, they would move his
filing cabinets or repair his door hinges after much sucking-
in of breath and with a poor enough grace. If he wasn't, they
would flatly refuse to help, listing fictitious prior commitments. But they were acutely sensitive to the slightest
nuance of company politics. They knew whether a man was
on the way up, sidelined, or on the way down, and acted
ruthlessly upon their perceptions. However, Mr Horrocks
was greeted in friendly enough fashion by the others
present, offered a chair and given a large mug of tea and a
copy of the Daily Mirror. He would be happy and safe for
an hour or so. His headache from the previous night's beer
could be nursed along gently and in peace.

The Mayor and Mr Muffle followed Sir Blathwell into a
scene of great contrast with the distant factory buildings.
The reception area was vast and splendid. It had a polished
marble floor which spread towards a distant marble-fronted

reception desk. Behind it sat two immaculately dressed, doll-like young women who exuded coolness and aloofness to all who dared approach. Like many of the people in the offices, neither of them had the faintest idea of how closely their salaries were related to the success of the men who made things in the factories.

They had little idea of the importance of the salesmen in the same office-block, all well-groomed, fast talking extroverts. The salesmen had to go out each day and unload the Company's products onto an increasingly reluctant market which was steadily finding cheaper and better alternatives being made in other places. Neither factory workers nor salesmen rated very highly at Blank's Bearings though the latter, being in the offices, did at least rate higher than the former.

The atmosphere of the reception area was almost cathedral-like. It demanded to be entered with reverence. Visiting salesmen from other companies crept in to be kept waiting for long periods by self-important middle-ranking managers who took delight in passing downwards some of the contempt which often landed upon them from above. They simply couldn't visualise a situation in which the salesman might get them out of a hole one day, if some vital supply ran short and they had invested in some goodwill and an occasional cup of coffee. Even less could they understand the reality that, in some enlightened companies, the best salespeople might get to the top of the management tree and wield real influence. Visiting salesmen had always been treated like dirt at Blank's. This was in stark contrast to the cheerful reception afforded to Mr Horrocks by the Company drivers in their room – but the idea of learning anything from the conduct of the Company drivers would have been regarded as bizarre.

At one time, the men from the factories had had to come through reception if they had problems with their weekly pay-slips. Mistakes were frequent but the anxiety of the men to have them rectified was always dismissed in casual fashion by the wages clerks who 'would put in right in next week's', little comprehending the immediacy of one's pay-packet to someone who has to buy food, or shoes for the

kids, or pay the rent the next day. But this accessibility had
been noted by Sir Blathwell who had quickly decided that
you couldn't have the workforce cluttering up the marble-
floored reception in its dirty overalls. A special side-
entrance had been made for them and their pay-packet
problems. Once inside, they were granted the privilege of
being addressed by the most junior female wages clerk who
spoke through a wire grill fixed just slightly higher than the
height of the average man. There were no seats for those
who might be waiting their turn.

So, as Sir Blathwell led his visitors through reception,
there were no factory workers in dirty overalls to offend the
eye. At one time there might have been a lot of people
talking about buying things made by the company. But
today, as on many other recent days, there were no buyers
either.

They puffed up a wide, circular staircase to the second
floor where the company gods, headed by Sir Blathwell,
had rooms of strictly graded magnificence. Miss Prewitt had
flustered on ahead and was there to push open the heavy,
solid oak door, so highly sprung to the closed position that
it would have been inconceivable to enter for a casual chat.
There would have had to be a very pressing reason. Sometimes even that wasn't enough if Miss Prewitt judged the
prospective visitor to be of insufficient importance. Sir
Blathwell was treated regally by those close to him and
protected ferociously from ordinary people.

On this occasion, the pressing reason was Sir Blathwell's
own and that had opened his door to the visitors. Despite
his casual attire, there was nothing at all casual about his
views on keeping Zugswang of Dusseldorf well away from
Standing Stillbury and his workforce.

He gestured to them to sit in front of his desk and took
his own leather-covered seat, slightly higher than theirs by
design, on the other side. The desk was vast and leather-
covered and not a piece of paper lay on it, nor was one visible anywhere else. It matched well with the oak-panelling
of the room, incongruous in this particular building, but
deemed essential for the Chairman of Blank's Bearings.

Miss Prewitt came in with freshly percolated coffee,

served in cups of the finest china bearing a floral pattern which had been named a century before in honour of the town whose future, or one facet of it at least, they were about to discuss.

The visitors were uneasy about starting the conversation but Sir Blathwell wasn't. He had neither delicacy nor tact.

'Look here', he opened, 'Meadows here (he nodded in the direction of the Mayor as he said this) has told me, in confidence of course, about this damn fool idea of getting the Zugswang project in the Town. I thought it right to let you know about the problems you are going to cause if you go on with this.'

'For a start, the damned road system won't take another large company. You know what it's like. All bloody stop-go and belching fumes as it is. And think of all that extra effluent pouring down the drains, straight through to the river and messing up the salmon fishing.'

When Sir Blathwell wasn't playing golf in company time, on the pretext of maintaining business contacts, he was salmon fishing on the River Septon, as the season permitted, for precisely the same reason. Company sales over several years showed no concrete result which might have been attributed to these activities.

'And,' he went on, 'Our whole way of life is going to be changed for the . . .'

At this point, Fred Meadows groaned inwardly. He had been over all this at least three times with Sir Blathwell who was supposed to talk about the damaging effects Zugswang might have upon wage levels at Blank's Bearings, not about problems for which Mr Muffle had already shown himself to have good answers.

Mr Muffle was about to spring into combat and demolish Sir Blathwell's arguments, but the Mayor, sensing this, put a restraining hand on his arm and, at the same time, leaned forward and interrupted Sir Blathwell's litany of imaginary dangers which were, by this time, being repeated in half the pubs in Standing Stillbury.

'If you, er, remember, Sir Blathwell, we have talked about those sorts of things, but I rather wanted you to explain about the wages problem.' He spoke deferentially, still far from sure of himself with someone who had both a title and a temper.

Sir Blathwell had a slight choking fit, brought on by a combination of being interrupted (unheard of), having forgotten his script (frequent, though seldom pointed out) and his difficulty in finding the right words (unusual) to explain to Mr Muffle the real problem faced by Blank's Bearings.

He glared but, after a moment, re-composed himself.

'Ah, yes, of course. Quite apart from all those things, you have to think about the effect on wage levels. As you know, er Miffle, Blanks have been the biggest employer in Standing Stillbury for years and years.'

'Yes', responded the Town Clerk, 'and it's Muffle, with a u.'

'Quite so, of course,' snorted Sir Blathwell like an angry Frisian bull, his eyes bulging slightly and taking on a rather red aspect at this correction following immediately upon an interruption. 'But the point is that times are very hard at the moment (times had been hard for Blank's Bearings for at least 40 years) and I can't have half my men rushing off to work for the wretched Bosche, er Germans you know, probably for twice the money, and then have wage rates shooting up as we try to keep them. It could finish us. Have you any idea what that could do for the economy of the Town?' As he said this, Sir Blathwell stood and looked fondly through the window down to the silver-grey Mercedes, still behind the Mayor's car at the foot of the steps.

Mr Muffle considered this question for a moment. He thought it might really mean 'What would it do for the economy of Sir Blathwell in the run-up to his retirement?'

The momentary silence whilst he thought through his answer appeared to irritate the questioner, whose hectoring manner usually made his employees feel compelled to answer questions instantly, with a consequent loss of clear thought and precision. Sir Blathwell sat down again and began to tap a pencil on the vast leather surface of the desk. He was not used to any show of coolness from those with whom he was locked in discussion.

Mr Muffle had come well prepared. Although a naturally polite man, he didn't have the Mayor's marked deference, common to all small-town social climbers, towards the titled. Mr Muffle's overwhelming virtue was that he had no social aspirations and thus didn't give a hoot for what people like Sir Blathwell thought of him.

'What it will do for the economy of the Town, Sir Blathwell, is this. To begin with, five hundred new wage packets will be emptying into the local shops and businesses – and that will only be the start. More money will filter from Zugswang into the wage packets of people at companies from which they buy small parts they can't make themselves. They are bound to buy locally if they can – it's usually cheaper. All that is bound to be good for Standing Stillbury. We can't actually stand still for ever and assume that there will never be much unemployment here. We have to move forward and start thinking about the future.'

There was a sort of hrumphing noise from Sir Blathwell whose red eyes had now taken a vaguely mad aspect. Mr Muffle continued.

'And as for the loss of your workforce, it won't happen like that. People aren't nearly as adventurous as you think. Some will be too set in their ways to move (like the whole wretched company, he thought to himself) and some will hate the idea of working for Germans. Some won't even be suitable for Zugswang: they'll be too old to train up for the new high-tech machinery. And if you do get a few going, I've more than a suspicion it might just save you some redundancies over the next year or so – it could even save you some redundancy payme ...

But before Mr Muffle could even complete the word payments, Sir Blathwell was rising from his chair, his face turning scarlet, his teeth bared in a snarl.

'What? WHAT in God's name do you know about redundancies? Who told you that? This is an OUTRAGE! You come here from the Town Hall to tell me about the economy of this town. The ECONOMY! You people couldn't run a whelk stall and you come to talk to me about the ECONOMY. All you people contribute is bigger bloody rate bills each year and a load of bureaucracy to get in the way of the people who really do something for the ECONOMY.'

As Sir Blathwell's face reddened, the volume of the word economy increased each time it was repeated. Mr Muffle inwardly conceded that Sir Blathwell's last comment had a certain basis in fact which he rather regretted. But by this time, the iron had entered his soul and his own eyes took on a steely glint to match the explosions coming from Sir Blathwell.

'So,' snapped the Town Clerk, 'there ARE redundancies on the way! That appears to have been the main contribution of Blank's Bearing to this town over the last ten years. Your company once employed five thousand people here – now you have about two thousand and the number's still dropping. And you wonder why I want some new blood injecting into the Town. You can't be serious.'

It was many years since anyone had told Sir Blathwell Scam that he couldn't be serious. The last one to do so had been sacked – but even Sir Blathwell Scam had no means of sacking the Town Clerk of Standing Stillbury.

There was a further terse exchange, Sir Blathwell remaining in his half-standing position, getting even deeper red in the face, the Mayor, quite ashen at a turn of events he had not expected, attempting to shrink into the recesses of his suit. A final suggestion by Mr Muffle that Blank's might even benefit by studying the new technology which Zugswang were sure to introduce seemed like a body-blow to Sir Blathwell who had by now become almost incoherent. The Mayor decided upon retreat at the moment when Miss Prewitt rushed accusingly into the room with a glass of water for her Chairman. He muttered apologies and attempted some calming words which Sir Blathwell seemed not to hear and dragged the Town Clerk out of the room. Miss Prewitt was hovering around him, in some panic, as they left.

Mr Horrocks had been watching from the drivers' portacabin and saw their approach early enough to be waiting ready at the car. On the way back to the Town Hall there was silence for a while. Then the Mayor, still shaken, spoke out. 'Bloody hell. Did you really have to get him going like that. I don't know if I can show my face in the Club for a month.' (In this, the Mayor was only half right. When word of the frightful meeting got around, some of the members would be rather amused and he and Mr Muffle would assume minor heroic proportions. Title or not, Sir Blathwell Scam wasn't everyone's cup of tea at the Conservative Club.)

Mr Muffle had remained quite terse himself. But whereas the Mayor's terseness was induced by simple fright, the Town Clerk's had been engendered by a battle in which he had, unusually, become quite angry.

'Look Fred,' he replied after his customary few seconds thought, 'The Man's a complete idiot and you know it. You have got to take control of this situation and decide without people like Blathwell Scam getting in your way. Are we going for the Zugswang project or not? And if not, how could you possibly justify it to the Planet? If you play it right and get all those jobs in this town, you'll end up with your statue in The Square – the first visionary we've had in this damn place in a hundred years. Think of it!'

The Mayor didn't know how he could explain to the Deepshire Planet. He remained silent. But the idea of the statue and being seen as a visionary was something he hadn't remotely considered. Not for the first time, the Town Clerk had shown him a new angle to a problem.

Perhaps firm leadership was needed – and to hell with the moaning from those who didn't quite have his qualities as a, what was the Town Clerk's word . . . visionary! That was it! He decided to think things through, carefully. He began to look a bit more cheerful, or, at least, a little less discomfited.

Mr Muffle had by now decided, come what may, to write his report to the Policy and Resources Committee with a recommendation that they try to get Zugswang in Standing Stillbury. They and the Mayor and the lot of them could chuck it out if they wanted. But by that stage they would have to do it in public and explain their decision. He could imagine how the national papers would love a story about protecting wage rates at a clapped-out company like Blank's Bearings. He thought, with a little malice, that he might set

up the Town Forum for an interview on local radio in which
they weighed up their vision of the Town against the
jobs which might be gained. They might just be laughed
off the air. But he had lost a month. Only an earthquake,
he thought, ever brought about special meetings of the
committees at Standing Stillbury Borough Council. The
members wouldn't recognise an economic earthquake if it
happened under their feet. He would have to wait for the
next meeting.

Chapter 4 – A Delegation

Within a day or so of Mr Muffle's unhappy meeting with Sir Blathwell, a delegation arrived in complete secrecy at the council offices in Concrete Hardening. It consisted of the Chairman of Zugswang Components, Herr Grossemann, his Finance Director, Herr Pfennig and Warren Clews-Lessly. They arrived in the Junior Industry Minister's official car.

Zugswang Components was a model of the German engineering industry. It was a family-owned company which had been founded at the beginning of the century by Herr Grossemann's grandfather. The company had survived the hyper-inflation of the twenties and the disasters of the second world war to emerge, completely re-equipped, as a leader in its field of automotive part production. Its contribution to armament production between 1939 and 1945 had been significant but sufficiently below the league of Krupp and Messerschmidt not to have caused any lasting image problem. The family had done its bit as loyal Germans but, with extraordinary foresight, avoided anything more than the most cursory contact with the party which ruled for the twelve years from 1933.

The Company was a heavy investor in new technology and high quality staff, upon whom more was then invested in continual specialised training. The shareholding remained almost exclusively within the Grossemann family. It was this autonomy which had made possible the rather un-German decision to look at a site abroad when the factory needed to be expanded beyond the capacity of its Dusseldorf site. British labour costs had fallen steadily below those in Germany and since half of the Company's products were going to British or British-based customers, the decision seemed entirely rational. The Chairman and the Finance Director looked like solid citizens to whom prudence in the management of the Company's affairs came naturally.

Herr Grossemann was tall, at least six feet two inches, heavy and straight-backed all at the same time. His clothes were sober, including the dark tie which revealed membership of the Kriegsmarine ex-Submariners' Association. At this early meeting at least, he didn't appear to be a man who smiled much. Herr Pfennig was shorter and much thinner, with those gold-rimmed spectacles with which British filmmakers always adorn Gestapo officers. He looked quite intense. Warren Clews-Lessly was, as usual, relaxed and dressed in a tweedy sort of suit and brown brogue shoes which might have been chosen for a day in the country. As a matter of fact, he considered that because Concrete Hardening was in Deepshire, his visit had, strictly speaking, to be classified as a day in the country. This might be a city in the making but that was all too recent to count against centuries of Deepshire being synonymous with agriculture, fox-hunting, rather good fishing and rough shooting. He grinned at the reception party as he emerged from his car with his guests.

The delegation was met by Henry Morgan, the Chief Executive, Mr Clamp the Planner, and Brian Fichtl. Ernie Truscott was busy at his own factory and had decided to leave the business to the other three, especially as the Chief Executive and Brian spoke German. In addition, matching three people with another three makes for an easier sort of day. They had consciously avoided the usual municipal bun-fight in which everyone of any position or self-esteem had to be included in a meeting with important visitors if howls of rage at a subsequent council meeting were to be avoided. At Concrete Hardening the Chief Executive and the political leaders were sufficiently united on this point that councillors, even the most pompous and self-important, had learned not to bother making a fuss if they were left out. Unusually in local politics, Ernie also trusted the others to get on with things and give him a full report of progress over dinner with the delegation that evening.

Introductions were quickly effected over coffee in Henry Morgan's office. Warren Clews-Lessly jokingly reminded both sides that he was present in a strictly neutral role, in support of the Government's determination to give every possible assistance to the smooth transition of Zugswang Components to their factory in the United Kingdom – wherever they happened to choose. The Concrete Hardening representatives nodded and smiled at this and made a good face of believing him – knowing full well that he wouldn't have been present if Concrete Hardening didn't already meet with government approval for the purpose. The real issue was whether it would suit Zugswang.

The introductions over, the party set out in a hired mini-coach to show their town to the guests. They would visit the Riverside Campus Site and another German company whose factory had already been in production for two years. The Germans quickly made it clear that they were almost as happy to speak English as their own language, so some of each flowed back and forth across the gangway of the 'bus. The sun even began to shine over the Summer greenery of the trees from amongst which the dazzling, glass-clad offices and the bright new factories protruded.

A day like this might have been thought a little difficult for Brian Fichtl. His parents had come to live in Concrete Hardening in 1939 – though it didn't have that name in those days. They had escaped from a part of Czechoslovakia which had become distinctly uncomfortable because of people of Herr Grossemann's nationality. However, it wasn't. That was all long ago and history was the last thing on the Councillor's mind. Even his now aged parents had reacted with a chuckle when he had told them what he would be doing that day – though he had not mentioned the name of the company, even to them. Brian ruefully observed to himself that his parents seemed to have shed their hatred of Germans quite easily. Yet he couldn't get some of his colleagues in the Labour Party to shed attitudes and policies dating from the first World War, let alone the second.

As usual on a day of this sort, of which Concrete Hardening had seen many, the talking during the coach tour was left mainly to Mr Clamp. His head had accumulated a vast amount of information about the factories on this or that side of the road as they passed. He could remember the names of many of the Japanese, German, French, Italian and British Managing Directors, the things their companies made, how many people they employed, the sort of things which had clinched their decisions to build factories in Concrete Hardening as opposed to anywhere else. He talked about the levels of pay in the different industries in the Town, the availability of workers and, to the surprise of the visitors, some of the problems which had been encountered by other foreign companies which had come before.

The Germans asked an occasional question, but mostly listened intently, pleased for once to be hearing hard facts instead of civic waffle about the town they were inspecting – and Concrete Hardening was one of several. Occasionally, if they had difficulty in grasping something said in Mr Clamp's Yorkshire-English, one of the other home players would quickly interpret.

Unknown to their hosts, the German delegation had made contact with friends in two of the other German companies already operating in the Town. The reports they had received were good and, although they reacted in non-committal fashion, they began to realise that Mr Clamp was giving them the complete truth. This, they guessed accurately, indicated a certain confidence in the product he was selling.

The Riverside Campus was quickly inspected. It was well above flood-level with the drains and services completed and ready for connection. There was nothing to stop building work starting tomorrow. The site was bounded by trees and shrubs and the only other factory buildings in sight were clean and modern: one of them made high-tensile springs of a type Zugswang Components used a great deal in their production of components.

This fact had been noted, quite independently, by both Zugswang itself (whose researchers had pored over a detailed map of the Town and its business directory some days before) and by Mr Clamp's staff in the Planning Department where they always liked to give their boss a few decent cards to play during meetings of this kind.

The emergence of this shared knowledge caused a mild

chuckle on both sides. Herr Grossemann, who had still not
said much, observed that if further research of this kind
were needed it might make sense for the two lots of staff to
get together in future. It was a promising start.

By mid-day they arrived at the doors of a German
company which was quite new to the Zugswang delegation.
Laufer Circuit Boards was a smallish outfit run by Herr
Springer. He himself had been enthusiastically recruited
into and welcomed by the business community of Concrete
Hardening and was always happy to share his pleasure at
that fact. In fact, he was standing at the front door of the
building, waiting to meet his visitors as the coach arrived, at
precisely the appointed time.

The building was obviously new and clad in green and
yellow metallic panels with porthole-shaped windows. The
name of the Company was proclaimed proudly on each of
the four sides of the factory in stainless steel letters fixed to
the panelling. It looked like something from the space age
which, indeed, it was. In contrast, the surrounding 20
metres or so of land were cultivated with a mixture of lawns
and garden beds in which displays of gladioli and irises
alternated rather splendidly. Someone was obviously being
paid to maintain the gardens in immaculate condition.

A brief tour of the factory revealed much about Herr
Springer and his ideals as a businessman. Of the 120
employees, 110 were employed in making, testing, packing
and delivering the circuit boards which went to customers
all around the UK and the rest of the European Community. The remaining ten, who included Herr Springer,
worked in an open-plan office organising the wages, sales,
invoices, advertising and anything else considered strictly
essential to the Company. There were no complex chains of
command. People were employed to do specific jobs and
did them, asking advice from or offering comment to anyone else they chose, including Herr Springer. On the other
hand, if someone was ill or on holiday, then someone else
filled-in for them.

Everyone, office worker, managing director, manual
worker, wore the same uniform which consisted of a simple
pale blue jacket with the company badge on the breast

pocket. Everyone had access to the managing director's desk – which was quite without protection from any dragon-like secretary or other kind of deterrent to communication and human relationship.

Of course, there were minor inconveniences in this arrangement. Another room had to be kept available for meetings which simply could not be conducted in public, so to speak. But the pay-off was considerable.

The people in the office felt close to the managing director – and that improved both morale and their self-esteem. He, on the other hand, could be sure that they had no opportunity to fritter away half the day on crosswords, reading magazines, chattering, arranging their social life, playing computer games, varnishing their finger-nails or any of the other hundred and ten activities which British office-workers regard as their birthright, to be practised in company time. Since the Company was busy anyway, the staff lost the inclination to do these things without even realising it.

The people in the factory, which was entered directly through a door from the open-plan office, were free to wander in and out if they wanted Herr Springer. But they seldom had the need. His practice was to spend at least half of each day on the shop-floor where he knew pretty well everyone by name. He also knew what they did and whether they were having any problems doing it. If they were, he didn't humiliate them with a public lambasting. He simply sat down with them over a cup of coffee and chewed things over until he found a way of getting round the difficulty. Since he had a way of talking on an equal basis, no-one found this method difficult to stomach and he invariably managed to get the best out of his people.

The system of quality control was also interesting. Everyone was on his or her honour to send nothing but a perfect piece of work from his own stage of the production process to the next. Furthermore, any employee on a production line was expected to press a button which stopped all further movement if he or she became aware of a technical problem developing. The effect of doing this was to sound a shrill whistle as a red light came on overhead. When this happened the Managing Director or his deputy would come to the problem point and help to rectify the fault.

Being given responsibility for stopping a production line and then not getting a rollocking for actually doing it, had been a painful experience for some employees, especially those recruited from the more archaic British companies. The idea of being in a position to control some aspect of their work was astonishing to those who had only been offered confrontation in the past. But they had got over the sleepless nights and come to terms with the frightening prospect of being regarded as intelligent human beings.

There was no separate quality control department. So far, not a single faulty circuit board had left the factory. Statistically, it might just happen one day. But by then the customers would know it for the fluke it would be and there would be no recriminations. And the responsible employee would neither be ridiculed nor blamed. There would simply be a painstaking discussion to work out how the fault could be prevented from recurring ever again.

And then there was the canteen. There was no special dining room for the company board and managers. They all ate in the same, spotlessly clean room and Herr Springer, made a point of sitting at a different table most days so that he could hear what, if anything, was going through the heads of the staff. This had also disconcerted the English employees for the first few weeks – but after a while they relaxed and got to chatting and joking with Herr Springer as if he were one of them – which he actually assumed he was.

The discussions would often shift towards the things the Company did, and how they might be done better, which was exactly what he wanted. Some members of the staff had been astonished to find their ideas being tried out. If they didn't work out, there were no moans – but if they did, the fact was very publicly acknowledged and reflected in the lucky employee's salary cheque that month – and they were all paid a salary, monthly, and by cheque.

Everyone at Laufer Circuit Boards felt valued by the Company's management. No-one had the dismal feeling of being treated like a number on a payroll, from whom the maximum amount of fair to indifferent work was bludgeoned in return for as little pay as could be got away with. In fact, the pay wasn't brilliant. The Company, which operated in a cut-throat market, didn't pretend otherwise. But being noticed as individuals, being listened to, being recognised and even shown respect by the Managing Director if he met them in the street with their families, all combined to produce a fierce loyalty amongst the Company's employees. Staff turnover was reduced to that small number of congenital malcontents who simply cannot fit into any place where actual work is expected in return for regular pay.

Lunch for the Zugswang delegation and the Council party was in the staff canteen with Herr Springer and some of his colleagues – some very junior. The Laufer staff had been asked to help look after the guests without pressing them on the precise reason for their visit. So they all enjoyed a pleasant meal during which the casual, uninhibited chat from some of the staff did nothing to diminish Herr Grossemann's increasingly favourable impression of what he was seeing. The Council people and the junior minister sat back contentedly and for the most part let the conversation flow between the German visitors and their company hosts.

After lunch, they all thanked Herr Springer warmly for his hospitality and strolled back towards the coach. Herr Grossemann, by now making little attempt to conceal his favourable impressions, asked if it was possible to see somewhere older, just for contrast, before some serious discussion got under way over dinner in the Concrete Hardening Hotel that evening.

'Well, yes', replied Brian Fichtl. 'There's a lovely old place just half an hour from here. Standing Stillbury. It even has a castle! Have you ever heard of it?'

Herr Grossemann and Herr Pfennig confessed that they had not – but that they would be delighted to have a look. So the coach quickly took them all to the ancient County Town of Deepshire. The traffic was a bit tedious on the way in but the Germans rather liked the cramped streets with buildings representing almost every period in the post-Roman history of British architecture.

They were especially delighted with the Castle, the 11th century red sandstone barrier at that one part of Standing Stillbury's ancient boundary which had not been guarded by the River Septon from incursions by the wild people from across the old border. Of course, the Town had spread well beyond the protective loop of river over subsequent centuries, its growth spawning a variety of stone and metal bridges at places where there had once been just ferry-boats. But even at this time their was a faint, residual whiff of superiority vested in living 'within the bridges'.

The Castle grounds remained accessible, for a small fee, before the planned re-opening ceremony. The main building was still closed but they were able to climb the steep stairway to the top of Queen Mathilde's Tower, the highest point on the turreted ramparts which surrounded the central bailey.

They looked around at the panorama presented by one side of Standing Stillbury from their historic vantage point. Beyond the hotch-potch of town centre streets was the Stills' football ground on the edge of the River, the Railway Station, half of which straddled the swirling current on its massive iron-column supports, and the Victorian villas and large houses which overlooked the River and Standing Stillbury Weir from the far bank. Life in the old houses, their gardens leading down to steps or even boathouses at the water's edge, must have been pretty agreeable on sunny afternoons in Victorian England when Standing Stillbury was the centre of life in Deepshire and half the map of the World was still coloured red. By the time of these events, both things had changed – but the villas and gardens still looked quite pleasant places in which to live, even if a shade seedy and perhaps occupied by people who could no longer afford to maintain them in quite the condition of their prime.

Clearly, Standing Stillbury was a rather charming, easy-on-the-eye sort of town to have within half-an-hour's drive of one's factory, perhaps even the sort of place in which to live whilst working in Concrete Hardening.

Then, without remotely considering that Standing

Stillbury might be in the market for the Zugswang factory, or Standing Stillbury having had any inkling of the visit taking place, the German delegation was taken back to Concrete Hardening to enjoy an hour's rest before meeting some more of that Town's councillors, of various political parties, over dinner.

The day had gone well.

Chapter 5 – The Member of Parliament Speaks

Back at Standing Stillbury, things were getting difficult for Mr Muffle.

He was, by invitation, sitting in on a completely unofficial meeting of the Council's Conservative Group, a strange mixture of folk. There were retired people who dreaded change of any kind, a few Town Forum members fiercely dedicated to preventing it, people who didn't work for a living but who seemed to have money, and assorted businessmen who claimed to regard council membership as their civic duty.

The businessmen, as opposed to the professional people, formed a part of Standing Stillbury society which could, in its turn, be divided into sub-categories, most of which were represented in the room.

There were the solid owners of old family businesses, cautious, straight-laced people who generally paid their rates and their debts first and spent on themselves only what was left. These people often ran shops, or small wholesale businesses, built house extensions for other people, just one or two at a time, employed a few others in activities like plumbing or furniture-removals – or even ran the odd small factory tucked away here or there in the backstreets of the Town.

They were sometimes second or third generation but seldom more. By that time, there would usually develop a strong conviction that the accumulated assets of their forebears and themselves were best spent on expensive private education for the children so they wouldn't have to do anything as demeaning as the said forebears. How wise this was, and how happy the next generation would be in consequence, were difficult to foresee. Nevertheless the people from this group usually had the best feel for Standing Stillbury. They had a sense of involvement and investment

in the place, often going back a long time. You could usually
trust them.

The second group was very interesting. This consisted
the first generation creators of new businesses. Inevitably,
some succeeded by dint of hard effort, or simple good luck.
Others flashed across the social firmament of the Town for
a while and then crashed spectacularly, disappearing from
sight.

In the latter event, the danger signals were always plain
to see. A year or two into the new enterprise with profits
flowing in, seemingly for ever, large and conspicuous commitments would be taken on. Big new cars, usually German,
would appear in a driveway leading to a large new house
which had been specially built with every conceivable com-
fort and extravagance. Peacocks were often the big problem
with this group. They would be installed in the new garden,
thus earning the deep hatred of their established neighbours
who both resented such a vulgar statement of nouvelle
richesse and even more the consequent rude awakenings
when the wretched birds began their raucous noise in the
very early dawn of Summer mornings. In the most extreme
cases a personal helicopter might appear.

No charity ball or sportsman's evening, black tie obligatory, would be complete without the new entrepreneur,
usually carrying a portable telephone and surrounded by
like-minded friends of short-term commitment. Quite often,
these things (the helicopter almost always) portended disaster. The social appearances would become a little fewer
('though some conspicuously brazened it out until the day
before they were finally put into liquidation), the odd
rumour would trickle through the Rotary Club, Lodge or
Round Table. Then would come the creditors' meeting and
the bitter recriminations of suppliers who stood to lose thou-
sands for their goods or services, infuriated at the memory
lapses which now greeted their questions about this or that
precise item of expenditure on company cars or the possible hiding-away of untraced cash.

What money which could actually be traced would all go
to pay the big-city accountancy firm which was handling the
liquidation, its partners tearing greedily at the remains of the

business like vultures feasting on a carcass. The expensive house would often be found to be wholly owned by the wife or trustees and therefore untouchable.

Some of the un-paid suppliers would be so badly damaged as to go out of business themselves in consequence, financial tragedy thus being visited upon whole families. Sometimes they then had the galling experience of seeing the malefactor swaggering through the Town having set up a completely new business to begin the whole dismal cycle over again. The astonishing thing was that some suppliers, knowing the risk, would actually do business with the wretch, counting on making more from him during the period of solvency than their likely loss if he self-indulged himself and his family into bankruptcy again.

But some of these people would make it to the last square of the snakes and ladders board of business life. They would get solidly established and make a real contribution to the Town by employing people and providing services or goods of real value to their customers. They would earn deserved respect from all who knew them. Then, a generation or so later, the family would be thinking about how they could get the children out of all that and into proper jobs like accountancy, law or merchant banking.

The third group was perhaps the least represented. It consisted of people who ran businesses for other people – often small chain stores with identical branches in almost every town. Not many of these people came on to the Council. For them, Standing Stillbury was simply one stage of a career taking in, perhaps, ten or fifteen towns, in each of which they would be faithful to the company oath to wear dark suits (even in bed), keep their hair cut short and combed flat, say nothing out of turn in public, and occasionally be pictured in the Deepshire Planet making a modest charity presentation to a local cause, always by means of a cheque measuring about three feet by eighteen inches to ensure that the readers were in no doubt about the name and immense generosity of the donor-company.

These creatures of British mass-retailing usually refused to decorate their shop fronts when Standing Stillbury was being judged in the annual Town of Flowers competition.

They gave the impression that their futures in their soulless, accountant-controlled, regulated-to-the-last-comma sort of organisations depended upon keeping their branch exactly like that in every other town in England and never being a single millimetre out of step. Ever.

Curiously, the managers of the really big national stores seemed much more inclined to enter into the life of the Town. Some clearly found it much to their liking and lost the urge to move on. But even they shunned Council membership, finding the talk to action ratio well beyond the blood-pressure zone.

A fourth group was quite unrepresented on the Council. This was the small number of people who ran very large industrial businesses in the area. They either didn't have the time or, in the cases of some, like Sir Blathwell Scam at Blank's Bearings, would never enter any arena in which they had to argue a case and then face a vote upon the outcome. It was interesting that some of Sir Blathwell Scam's factory employees had gained election to the Council as Labour members (in a minority it must be remembered) for the sort of reasons which kept Sir Blathwell away. Compared with Blank's Bearings, the Council was a place where other people, even the Conservatives, listened to them, argued with them fairly rationally and, occasionally, if the issue wasn't too party-political, even agreed with them.

But Mr Muffle faced only Conservatives, the ruling party, on this occasion. And, quite unofficially as usual, Member of Parliament Jack Fudge had been invited along as well.

The Mayor, Fred Meadows, had dithered and then decided that open disagreement might be too damaging if Mr Muffle just produced his report on Zugswang and sent it out with the Policy Committee agenda. He didn't want a situation in which the Labour members, traditional haters of industry and opponents of capital investment, appeared to show foresight and commitment to the future whilst his own people appeared in a bad light, opposing a bid for Zugswang for reasons which could hardly be trumpeted in public.

And he had been thinking more and more about the Town Clerk's comments on the way back from Blank's

Bearings. Perhaps he could emerge as a visionary in support of the new factory. But he would make damn sure that he wasn't alone in his own party. He had called the group meeting to put his toe gently into that bowl of acid.

However, there was one small item of business which the Group wished to discuss in this private forum beforehand – a matter which had soured public life in Standing Stillbury for some months: what to do about the freemasons.

The masons were not, as such, a real problem. They didn't fix Council contracts for their friends, they didn't appear to influence Council staff appointments in favour of other masons and those with an IQ in double figures didn't make any great effort to conceal the fact that they were masons. In fact, they were not required by Masonic rules to conceal their membership – only the mumbo-jumbo secrets of the organisation. And by this time, most of them were able to laugh at the mumbo-jumbo, privately, even with non-masonic friends. And there was hardly anyone still alive in the Town, perhaps just a few elderly Catholic ladies, who still believed that the Devil personally attended masonic meetings, with a special hole cut into the back of his dinner-suit trousers to allow his tail to poke through!

But the trouble was that non-masons, in all parties but mostly Labour which didn't have so many masons as the Tories, felt uneasy about having members of a nearly- sort-of secret society lurking amongst themselves. They couldn't quite put their finger on why – but every few years an irruption of concern would break into the public life of the town and a more or less hysterical burst of anti-masonic chattering would be the visible symptom.

And this time it was serious: the Labour Party was putting up a motion that required masons who were councillors or council employees to sign a register to that effect. The register was to be open to public and, in natural consequence, journalistic inspection.

This had proved highly divisive. The masons thought it was discriminatory. Half the Tory non-masons tended to agree but feared the voters might misunderstand their concern. The other half were as resolutely anti-mason as the Socialists – and the Socialists were by now sitting back laughing at the discomfiture of the Tories. The Liberals were trying to formulate an alternative policy which would offend no-one and please everybody. They would eventually sort their own views out about a year later, by which time local discussion would have shifted to dogs fouling footpaths (equally un-resolved) and no-one would be interested any more.

After some minutes of discussion, most of it supported by the usual unsubstantiated claims and counter-claims and a few of the standard bits of masonic baby-eating, blood-drinking, woad-smearing, conviction-quashing mythology, Fred Meadows, who was neither a mason nor anti-masonic – but who was tired of the issue, played his trump card.

'Gentlemen,' be began, 'It seems to me that we are approaching this problem from the wrong direction.'

'Even as a non-mason, I understand how members of the, . . . er, craft, might resent being forced to sign some sort of register. There really is too much Big Brother mentality in an idea like that – typical socialism if you ask me.'

'I don't think we should push on with this register idea at all.' There were groans from some parts of the room. 'I think that the answer is much simpler' – this said with an air of near-certainty and, most unlike the Mayor, something approaching a triumphant smirk.

Since the Mayor was not usually this confident in his pronouncements on difficult issues, the chattering slowly died away, faces turned towards him with a certain curiosity and everyone began to listen.

'The answer', continued the Mayor, 'is this' – at which he pulled from his left-hand jacket pocket a one-inch-long thin steel pin, on the end of which was a small, royal blue lapel badge, a plain disc measuring no more than a quarter of an inch in diameter – about the size of a Rotary or Round Table badge in fact.

'If the masons', the Mayor went on, 'are offended by being identified, we simply ask all the councillors and staff members who aren't masons to wear one of these! What could be simpler or fairer?'

There were a few seconds of silence as the meeting tried to digest this astonishing, clean solution to the problem. No-one had ever come up with anything like this before.

'Where did you get the badge?' asked one of the masonic councillors, desperately playing for time whilst he tried to think through the Mayor's idea.

'It was easy', replied the Mayor, 'I wrote to one of those companies that's always advertising promotional key-rings and things like that. They sent me this sample and said they could make these for 15p each.'

The silence deepened to total silence. Several minds now attempted to compute the possible consequences of the using the badges. Could they be sold throughout the whole country so that an entire national problem could be resolved by letting non-masons identify each other at a glance? Since most non-masons would be happy to admit to the fact – except those desperate to join but still uninvited – would the use of the badges really be identifying the masons by default, using a rather sneaky trick? Would some masons buy the badges themselves to cause confusion? If they did, what would other, non-badged, masons think of them? Could you have a badge with, for example, a gold dot in the middle to show that you were not a mason but were anxious to be invited in?

It was all too much to fathom. There was no clear response from anyone. The room began to buzz with a subdued sort of noise caused by very small groups of people trying to find out what the others thought without committing themselves first. It was suggested that the matter should be deferred for further thought – during which process it was destined to become a rare topic of council business which captivated the whole town for a week or so. Great debate on the badge idea would take place in saloon-bars and the drawing rooms of large houses alike. Like much else in Standing Stillbury it would remain unresolved. But for the moment, the Conservative Group decided to get back to the question of the new factory.

Councillor Albert Brown opened. He was a stalwart of the Town Forum who had never in his life supported anything new unless it bore directly and positively upon his financial interests. He regarded novelty with deep suspicion, as dangerous and bound to change things for the worse. The Councillor, like Ring Lardner, had known hunger as a young man, but had always managed to get to a good restaurant in time. He was now the senior partner in an estate agency which had been founded by his grandfather. He had never known family life outside a comfortable house with a large garden and a gardener. He took himself a shade seriously and was not noted for his humour. The year before these events a series of maliciously funny jokes about estate agents had circulated around the town, repeated regularly, to howls of alcoholic laughter, by speakers on the local after-dinner circuit. He had detested that and had not been able to conceal his pleasure when, after a few months, bankers became the new targets. When that happened his sense of humour had developed considerably.

The fortunes of Albert Brown's estate agency, which handled offices and shops more than houses, had been maintained through good times as well as bad. In good times the price of property and the commissions went up and in bad times it was still said to be going up.

In the latter event, he might be forced to negotiate downwards by the sharper and more alert in-coming tenants, but would only agree to their demands if they, in turn, agreed under strict contract, never to reveal the sums involved to a third party. Albert Brown could then claim, never directly but by strong hints, that the demanded rent levels had actually been achieved and use them as a starting point for other negotiations. The less sharp, more naive new office tenants would sometimes believe him and pay up. Even if they didn't, a dangerous downward spiral of rent levels, in favour of the tenants, was at least reduced in its force. Large sections of Standing Stillbury's commercial premises were thus deemed in public to be achieving rent level X per square foot when, in fact, they were secretly achieving the lower rent level Y.

'Mr Chairman', he began, 'I really don't know why we have to have this debate every few years. We have managed to keep Standing Stillbury as beautiful as any town in England (some listeners at this point wondered silently if Councillor Brown had forgotten his own professional involvement in the demolition of the beautiful Eagle Hotel and its replacement by a blank-fronted chain store a few years earlier – but that, they supposed, had been business) and we still have to talk about this or that company getting in here with a dirty, smelly factory and jobs nobody wants. They'll clog up the roads, chuck their rubbish down the drains and mess up our whole way of life here. Think of the image of the Town, why...'

For the second time in a week, the Mayor groaned inwardly. Could no-one grasp the essentials of the issue? They were all obsessed by roads and bloody drains.

'Look', he interjected testily. 'The roads and drains aren't the problem. If the factory comes here the roads and drains can be sorted out easily enough – it would pay us to do it. You must have heard that fact ten times already. It's the image of this Town that IS the problem. If we keep on doing nothing we'll end up as a museum of mediaeval England – nice to look at and the only work outside shops and offices will be dressing up in Civil War costumes and prancing round the Castle grounds for the tourists. The problem – so I am told repeatedly – is what would Zugswang do to the wage rates at the companies – and one specific company – we already have here? That is the issue and we shouldn't be wasting time on things which can be fixed. Do you or don't you approve of competition creeping in on manual workers' wage rates?'

Councillor Brown's jaw dropped slightly, in part because the Mayor was not known as a man who got passionate about very much and in part because he saw an obvious trap in answering the last question. Fred Meadows, after the non-Masonic lapel-pin idea and now this, was beginning to appear in a different light.

Before the Councillor could answer, some loud mumbling noises from the far side of the room suggested, without quite committing the thought to clear words, that competition in wage rates certainly wasn't wanted.

Looking intently, for he was rather short-sighted even with the end-of-the-nose spectacles, the Mayor recognised a few members of the Conservative Club who were especially friendly with board members at Blank's Bearings

– or Blank's Earrings as the missing letter was causing them to be referred to around the Town.

Councillor Brown, by now re-composed, chose to ignore the issue of wage rates and ploughed on with his theme of Standing Stillbury not being 'That sort of town'.

But then, just as the Mayor was beginning to regret coming so close to support for The Town Clerk's plan, he found the Councillor getting some sharp questions and an occasional heckle from another quarter.

Those present who kept shops which they also owned had taken a long time to reach a conclusion. It was always that way in Deepshire. But some of them had finally grasped that five hundred new wage packets in the Town, every week, might mean more money going through their tills. They weren't going to say that they were interested in the money going through the tills, of course. But they had, it seemed, developed a sudden, wider understanding of the needs of Standing Stillbury.

It was remarkable really. They started coming up with expressions like, 'What about the people who want jobs?' and 'We can't assume we have low unemployment here for ever.' and 'Standing Stillbury has to change with the times!' This last statement was greeted with astonishment by some of those present.

Quite a debate began to froth up as two sides more or less emerged and some of the fence-sitters began to ease themselves one way or the other, whilst not quite letting their feet touch the ground yet.

But after a few minutes more, in a small silence, Jack Fudge stood up and demanded by gesture the attention of all present. He had so far listened in glum silence.

'Ladies and Gentlemen', he began importantly, 'I want to thank you for letting me sit in on your group meeting this afternoon. I have thought long and hard about this issue myself and you might as well know that I think it would be a disaster for this Town if Zugswang Components set up their factory here. You can argue about the pros and cons all day but you all know in your hearts that we simply don't want any more industry in Standing Stillbury and I tell you bluntly, this company will come over my dead body!'

Loud cheers started up from parts of the room, to die in slight embarrassment at the silence with which this statement was greeted by those who had warmed to the idea of the new factory.

'Perhaps', thought some of the now silent new supporters of industry and jobs, 'we have been a bit hasty. Perhaps we really are in the minority.'

'Perhaps', thought some of the stronger-minded, 'we really do need a new Member of Parliament.'

But there was no more open debate. The meeting began to break up. In the corridor outside, they re-formed into small groups which re-ran the whole discussion in heated fashion. This was the point when people felt able to say, semi-privately, what they had REALLY felt – what, in fact, they should have had the courage to say during the meeting. They would begin their sentences with 'Of course, I couldn't say this in there but . . .' It's a great pity that no system has ever been devised for amending the minutes of meetings to reflect what people really think as revealed by the discussions which take place in little clusters afterwards.

Back in the Mayor's Parlour, Fred Meadows threw his papers onto the table. He was unhappy. Despite the Member of Parliament's clear declaration, this was still an unresolved piece of Council business. Nothing had been decided and controversy was on the way. There were no good grounds upon which to ask Mr Muffle to suppress his report. Without ever discussing the matter so directly, he realised well enough that Mr Muffle would have used his right as Town Clerk to report upon the matter anyhow. So he caved in gracefully.

'OK, OK, We aren't going to button this up before Policy and Resources. You'll have to let them get at each other's throats at next week's meeting and see what happens. Just let me see the final copy before the agenda goes out, if you have time.'

Mr Muffle happily agreed to this small courtesy and began putting his mind to the next day's royal visit.

Chapter 6 – A Great Day
for Standing Stillbury

The committee clerks, working in the garret-like top-floor
rooms of the Town Hall, had patched together all the details
of the ceremonial re-opening of the Castle by Princess
Mary. They had grumbled, as they always did, about it
interfering with their day-to-day task of organising the work
of the council committees. They had even put in hours of
overtime, for which they were not paid. But they would
have been outraged if the job had been given to anyone
else.

For no very good reason but the human delight in being
privy to secret goings-on, the whole matter of a royal visit
was always treated as something of the utmost confidentiality for as long as possible. The fact of the impending visit
was first of all concealed for un-defined reasons and then,
when that got out, the detailed organisation was kept
behind firmly closed doors. Everything was confined to the
small circle of Mr Muffle and the committee clerks who
relished this small accretion of power. It gave them a feeling
of importance and mystery. Even Internal Audit had no
acceptable reason for demanding details in advance – and
would have been rebuffed gleefully had they done so.

They all came in to the office at 8.00 am on the day.
They had to go through everything, with the Town Clerk,
for the tenth time. They left nothing foreseeable to go
wrong. There was always something unforeseeable but that
couldn't be avoided.

Mr Muffle sat at the top of the conference table in his
spacious room, overlooking the River Septon, and questioned them about this or that small point. Miss Peeves
fussed in and out with coffee from time to time. She
considered royal visits her and Mr Muffle's preserve and
the committee clerks as interlopers – but since the organisation of this or any other event was quite beyond her, she

had to accept their presence with no more than implied complaint. She would, of course, criticise the arrangements when the visit had finished but, in the meantime, simply made the point that she was one of the small group allowed to know everything. The others took no notice of her.

They considered the royal route through the Town. Had the men from the Works Department swept the streets? Had the usual harvest of illuminated bollards been kicked over by homeward-rolling young drunks the night before? Had the crowd barriers all been put in place along the pavement edges? Everything was reported as being in order.

They checked the speeches for the re-opening of the Castle. They had a last look at the luncheon menus and hoped that the caterers wouldn't make a mess of it this time.

The guest lists were the biggest problem. Those who had accepted their invitations had been carefully fitted into the seating plans for lunch. But there were always some who would never bother to reply but nevertheless turn up and make an enormous fuss if they weren't admitted. At least two of Standing Stillbury's Councillors fitted into that category. There would be a few who had accepted and wouldn't bother to turn up on the day. Some, of middle-ranking importance, who had been invited as individuals, would be sure to turn up with their wives or even business partners, and try to bully the staff on the gates into letting them both in. That ploy usually worked for anything but a royal visit. In this case they wouldn't be allowed and there would be more frightful scenes. But they would cope with all that.

They chuckled over the miraculous recovery from bronchitis of the chain-smoking Chief Medical Officer, whose wife had clearly decided that SHE was going to be presented to the Princess if it killed HIM. (It wouldn't).

The timing of every stage of the day was re-checked.

Those detailed to oversee it reported upon the preparation of the castle rooms, even down to the re-furbishment of the royal lavatory – an important matter upon which a good deal of money had been spent.

All sorts of people from the Council's various offices had been allocated to this or that position in and around the

Castle to make sure that the correct thing happened at the right moment – or even to see that the Councillors and guests parked well away from the Castle and didn't try to drive into the grounds – and some were sure to try that unless firmly stopped.

There was a myriad of such things to be grasped. But by 9.30 am they all knew what was expected of them and set out to get everyone else into position over the next hour or so.

The junior members of staff would be at the more distant stations, tense and nervous for their first royal visit. The more senior and experienced would be nearer to the centre of events where a firmer hand might be needed at some point. They would be more relaxed, knowing that if anything hadn't been fixed by then, it was too late anyhow. Once a royal visit started it was like a large stone rolling down a hillside. You more or less had to watch it go.

Mr Muffle himself, like the Mayor and Miss Peeves, (the last decked out in a new red outfit, black trimmed and with a matching three-cornered hat – at the same time both splendid and preposterous) would join the entourage of the royal party to show them around the Castle and its flower-bedded grounds before lunch. After lunch would come the ceremony at which the expensively re-furbished relic would be re-opened for the public and the tourists who thronged Standing Stillbury in Summer.

By this time, the approaches to the Castle were lined three or four deep with people who wanted a glimpse of the royal visitor. There were groups of schoolchildren who had been issued with small union flags to wave as the procession of cars passed. In past times there might have been more children but by the year of 19-- not so many teachers automatically brought children out to see royal visits. Some of them even disapproved and refused their invitations to do so.

The policemen were taking sniffer dogs around the castle grounds, ostensibly in a final check for explosives but actually to find out where they might wheedle a cup of tea out of the catering staff.

Princess Mary, in a deep purple Rolls Royce escorted by

three police cars, was due to arrive at the outskirts of Standing Stillbury at precisely 11.00 am. The fact of her arrival at this point would be signalled to the Castle by police radio so everyone would know he had seven minutes in which to get ready. The whole of the day was planned around that arrival time of 11.07 am. Most of the guests and the younger Council staff assumed that was how it would happen. Mr Muffle knew otherwise and was quite relaxed when the first message indicated that the Princess was running half an hour late. She was enjoying a visit to the school which formed the first part of her day's itinerary. The school happened to be just within the boundary of Concrete Hardening, a few miles along the road.

The Town Clerk barely raised his eyebrows when the next message estimated a delay of 45 minutes for the same reason. 'Par for the course', he thought to himself as those of less experience grew steadily more excitable.

Most people assume rightly that the Royals, with the one grumpy exception, love children and that is why school visits often run late. They do. They love the fact that children talk to them uninhibitedly. Small children make the royals laugh by being unselfconscious and outrageous, saying things which would cause sharp intakes of breathe coming from adults. So, the royals take their time in infant schools and then grit their teeth to be fawned over during the rest of the day when they encounter a succession of never-to-be-met-again civic and business leaders, most of them dull as felt boots. You have to allow for this during royal visits.

The Princess finally arrived at the outskirts of town at 11.51 am and the word quickly spread around those gathered in and outside the Castle grounds. The tour of the grounds would now have to be abandoned if the whole day were to be kept roughly on schedule. 'No loss there', reflected Mr Muffle who found the planning and control of these occasions a matter of personal satisfaction, but inclined to be tedious if they went on too long. He wasn't particularly for or against royalty and simply made private judgments on such individuals of that small category as he met. He gave the necessary orders to delete the walk around the grounds. It wasn't a problem. The committee clerks were used to improvising.

By this time the various lines of people who were waiting to be presented were getting restless and one in particular was becoming a problem, or rather two problems.

It was the first line. The one which happened to include no less than Henry Morgan, Chief Executive of Concrete Hardening District Council. It should be explained that Standing Stillbury Borough Council had no wish at all to be including people from Concrete Hardening in events of this kind. But they had been given no choice. Colonel Haugh, the Lord Lieutenant and representative of the Monarch in the County of Deepshire, had insisted they invite him to the lunch. The school previously visited by the Princess, being within the boundaries of Concrete Hardening, a civic presence from that Council was mandatory.

This was a messy arrangement, arising from the fact that local councils had one set of areas whilst Lord Lieutenants presided over royal visits for entire counties. So, occasionally, people had to be brought together who preferred not to talk to one another. Standing Stillbury had grudgingly done what it had been told. Henry Morgan had been invited to the lunch and to be presented to the Princess. He had been greeted with transparently false bonhomie by the senior officers of Standing Stillbury, who knew him, and ignored by most of the elected members, who did not.

But Henry Morgan's line for presentation, consisting of eight people, was being re-arranged from within by Councillor Jervis Boddington, a local accountant whose firm operated a rigid and ruthlessly pursued policy of paying no bill earlier than three months after receipt whilst demanding payment of its own bills within fourteen days – and harrying clients by telephone to ensure that they paid.

Jervis Boddington's career aims having been either achieved or abandoned, he had done what many successful businessmen in Standing Stillbury do at a certain point in their careers. From outside, he had regarded the Council as a hotbed of waste and profligacy which employed useless people to sit around doing very little for inflated salaries – salaries which, moreover, came from his enormous rates bill which increased faster than inflation, year after year.

So he, Jervis Boddington, had resolved to get elected and save the Town from this money-consuming monster.

The first part was easy. He was quickly found a safe Conservative seat in one of the leaf-mouldy suburbs and was elected to great acclaim – most of it self-generated by his plans to cut the rates.

The second part was impossible. Like many council crusaders before him he found that the organisation was already cut to the bone. The merest hint of further savings, when he got to actual details and specific services which might lose out, brought howls of protest from self interest groups around the Town – many of them powerful middle-class self-interest groups with members in the suburb which had elected him to cut OTHER people's demands upon the Council's resources, not their's.

But he had not quite lost all his illusions and had not yet been sidelined out of harm's way by this stage. So he had been pleasantly surprised to be elected leader of the Conservative Group, a classic compromise choice who found himself sitting between two candidates of reasonable quality whose mutual hatred would have resulted in the election of either splitting the local party asunder.

This unforeseen success made him de facto leader of the Council – an expression he had first assumed to mean rather more than it did. For a start, he had been taken aback to find that the role of leader involved him in many of the Council's political affairs but left him playing a poor third fiddle to the Mayor on ceremonial occasions. That was not what he had expected at all. So whilst the Mayor would glory in escorting the royal visitor around the Castle, he, Jervis Boddington, was to be merely stuck in a line to be presented. In the best traditions of local party politics, Jervis Boddington detested the Mayor, a colleague in his own party, as a small shopkeeper of no intellect, breeding or background.

There is seldom much significance attached to the order in which people are lined-up to be presented to a royal. But being the man of action he was, Jervis Boddington decided that the Leader of Standing Stillbury Borough Council should be at the head of his line, not in third place after the Borough Treasurer, Mr Tite, and a much longer-serving councillor of no particular note.

So he started to re-organise them and, after some confused bickering during which he prevailed, everyone had changed position – and he was now first.

The young committee clerk detailed to get everyone into the proper order, and keep them in it, was too deferential. He tried to get everyone back into place but was quickly faced down by the Councillor. He might have been more persistent had he understood the danger involved in what had happened – but he didn't. Henry Morgan, who had somehow been moved from fourth to seventh place understood all too well – but confined himself to a quiet smile at what was about to follow.

But his expression of amused indifference quickly changed when two Standing Stillbury Councillors, previously placed next to each other but now on either side of him, continued what had obviously been a long, confidential chat about a meeting the previous day. They had no idea who Henry Morgan was. But they seemed to be talking about a new German factory which might be built at the North End of Standing Stillbury. They seemed to suggest that the local Member of Parliament, Jack Fudge, was dead against it but that the Council might just decide to vote for it. That was the second problem caused by Councillor Jervis Boddington's re-arrangement.

Mr Muffle, standing besides the Mayor, spotted the illicit re-shuffle and started to stride over, well able to insist, in clear terms, that they should get back in place. But at that moment the police escort flashed blue-lit into view and everyone stood to attention, all eyes straining in the direction of the entourage. Mr Muffle hesitated, raised his eyes briefly to Heaven, and turned on his heel to re-join the Mayor.

This is the point in a royal visit when control is lost completely. The stone starts to roll down the hillside. You hope you have done enough work in the preparation.

As carefully planned, the members of staff detailed to step forward to open the doors of the cars in the royal entourage began to do so – and were brushed aside by the Special Branch Officers who appeared from the police cars and held the doors open themselves. This almost always happens as Mr Muffle knew very well, but you had to plan for your own people to be there or the law of perversity would one day leave the cars standing, doors unopened, in an embarrassed silence.

The Princess stepped out gracefully, clad in an elegant lemon yellow suit with a matching wide-brimmed hat. Her face radiated smiles. Internally, she was gritting her teeth and hoping against hope that she might be about to meet someone who was inspiring or interesting.

She was followed by two Ladies-in-Waiting, a couple of well-connected squirearchy wives from the home counties who knew which knives and forks to use and who enjoyed gathering up the bunches of flowers which are showered upon visiting princesses, making sure that the royal loo can be found and generally smoothing the way. The really good ones are hardly visible, unless the royal visitor is in some way threatened or inconvenienced, in which case they become rather more visible.

The Lord Lieutenant stepped out of the first police car and the various other members of the party stepped down as well. Mr Muffle and the Mayor stepped forward, hesitating slightly as they awaited the departure of the cars to get them from their position between the eager, assembled guests and the royal party. This had been carefully planned beforehand with the Chief Constable. The cars didn't move. Driver number one sat stolidly in position, either having forgotten or not having been told. Frantic gestures from the Chief Constable went unheeded. The cars were staying put. It was all fairly predictable.

The hesitation had been of a few second's duration. Mr Muffle, to whom very little was new, accepted the inevitable, steered the Mayor forward, the Lord Lieutenant introduced the pair of them and Miss Peeves hovered importantly in the near background so as to be sure that her relatives would see her on the television news that evening. The Princess received them all as if she hadn't been so charmed for a month. Whatever her innermost feelings, this wasn't one of the 'what, not another bloody civic party?' sort of royals. Princess Mary was, if one can say it of a royal, a professional.

The guests, who could see little of this across the tops of, or through the gaps between the cars, were a bit miffed but someone suggested, quite wrongly, that this was a vital security measure. The information quickly spread by concentric murmurs right through the crowd and was happily seized upon as a good reason for the cars remaining in place, having grown to a possible assassination attempt by the time it reached the outer edges. Some of the guests would be telling their grandchildren, many years later, that when they saw Princess Mary at the Castle the police cars had had to stay in place, between her and the crowd, as a security measure in the face of armed terrorists. But it was just a minor cock-up, nothing more.

Then they reached the first line for presentations. These presentations are the high point of any royal visit for most of the individuals involved.

Lots of people get to meet and even talk to royal visitors on a fairly casual sort of basis as they are shown through a factory or hospital or whatever. But if you have been stood in a line, with your name placed upon a special list beforehand, and then been formally presented by the Mayor or the Lord Lieutenant, that is something quite different entirely. You have been recognised as having some degree of importance. You have been PRESENTED, not merely introduced. The difference is keenly appreciated in places like Standing Stillbury and even, it must be said, in places like Concrete Hardening.

The procedure is smooth enough. The Lord Lieutenant and the host, the Mayor in this case, carry a copy of the list of names and one or other reads them off as the party walks along the eager line, the royal being pleasant to and exchanging a few inanities with the people who are being presented.

But the essence of the thing is to get the right names with the right people. Which is why it is dreadfully important not to change the order of the line. So the folly of Councillor Boddington began immediately to bear its crabby fruit –

especially as, by chance, the lead was taken by the Lord Lieutenant who didn't know many of the local councillors and officials, rather than by the Mayor, who did.

Councillor Boddington himself, proudly accentuating his rather puffed-out shape at the beginning of the line, was dismayed to be introduced as the Borough Treasurer. The Borough Treasurer, now at position 2, was quite put out to be referred to as Councillor Amos Dawes, whilst Councillor Dawes was rather flattered, at first, to be fussed over some-what – only to realise that he had been introduced as the Leader of the Council and that his name was now Jervis Boddington. However, the elderly Councillor Dawes, a long-retired stoker in the Royal Navy, had learned much better than the others to enjoy the fruits of life in relaxed fashion as they fell from the trees – so he quite enjoyed his un-planned prominence in the proceedings.

The rest of the line was quickly disposed-of, with Councillor Fred Jones, a rare Socialist on Standing Stillbury Council, representative of the North End Estate, bemused at becoming the Chief Executive of Concrete Hardening and the real Chief Executive hugely amused to be introduced as Councillor Basil Beardwell.

No-one even considered correcting any of this. The Princess was happily oblivious to the problem and the victims of the unintended insults to their local standing, who were seething in anger, instinctively felt it would be better to wait until she was out of earshot and then vent it on Councillor Jervis Boddington. In this small judgment they were quite correct.

Mr Muffle, The Mayor and Miss Peeves had moved on with the royal party. They had been all too aware of what had happened but Mr Muffle accepted it as a minor hic-cough on a day which was generally going quite well. Miss Peeves, though, when fortified by the wine which would be served with lunch, would make sure that the errant Councillor understood the enormity of what he had done.

But the very moment the presentations on his line had been completed, Henry Morgan, pleading indisposition, skipped the luncheon party, left the Castle grounds, and drove straight back to his office. No one missed him very much. They hadn't wanted him there in the first place.

The day went on without him.

The Princess endured thinly-sliced ham accompanied by some tired-looking salad. There was a modest Reisling from a part of what was then Yugoslavia. The waitresses were under strict orders, for financial reasons, to serve a single glass, and no more, per guest, though Miss Peeves had a private arrangement which would circumvent this stricture in her case. The Princess, sticking to a rule rigidly observed by most Royals whilst on duty, drank water. She might need a large gin back at the Palace that night – but that was another matter.

She pleasantly exchanged small talk with the Mayor and those local notables who had been accorded the biggest honour of all by being seated at her table. Then, at the end of lunch, she was escorted to the entrance where she was to unveil a plaque to commemorate the grand occasion of her re-opening Standing Stillbury Castle.

There were speeches, kept brief on the strict and sensible orders of the Lord Lieutenant, and then the Princess stepped back to pull the cord which would unveil the plaque.

The unveiling mechanism (which had been used for every plaque-unveiling in Deepshire for some years, passed around the various councils as need dictated) had been fixed to the Castle wall about five feet from the ground. Immediately below was a rectangular tub of assorted petunias in full bloom, placed there by the council gardeners at Mr Muffle's request. It looked delightful.

The Princess, smiling, pulled the cord and the expectant crowd burst into cheery applause which immediately died. Someone laughed out loud but quickly stifled himself. Then there was a subdued burble of puzzled and excitable chatter. There was no plaque behind the curtains.

The whole scene and what followed was repeated on every national and regional television news programme that evening. The following day the national newspapers ran sequences of pictures in comic-strip fashion. The stunned silence. The Mayor and Town Clerk stepping forward with looks of disbelief. Miss Peeves quickly retreating out of sight for the first time during the entire day. The sudden dawning of understanding. The retrieval of the plaque from behind the tub of petunias where it had fallen overnight. The saving of the day by the laughter of the Princess who, at last, after years of hoping, finally had something to remember with amusement from a civic visit. Her obvious good grace over the incident quickly infected the crowd which felt able to laugh as well. But Mr Muffle was furious, and so was the Mayor.

So after the Princess had left the Castle, to tumultuous applause made more heartfelt by her cheery humour, a private discussion was convened in Mr Muffle's office back at the Town Hall. A chastened Borough Surveyor was told in icy terms that Standing Stillbury had been made a national laughing stock and that a basic rule of civic life was that plaques were always screwed to walls, not stuck with some new-fangled epoxy resin, no matter how good the manufacturer's rep said it was. With his tail between his legs, the Borough Surveyor scuttled off to his office to repeat the message to the responsible member of his own staff, but in less decorous language than that used by Mr Muffle. But the Castle was now open.

Chapter 7 – Into Action

It took Henry Morgan just forty minutes to get back to the glass-clad office at Concrete Hardening. In twenty minutes more he assembled Brian Fichtl, Ernie Truscott and Mr Clamp, the planner. He explained, with some surprise in his voice, that Standing Stillbury was considering a bid for Zugswang.

'I can't make it out at all', he said. 'They don't usually know about our new factories 'til six months after we've had the official opening.'

'Now, I gather, they've a special Policy and Resources next week – and their Town Clerk is recommending they go for it. That idiot Fudge is apparently dead-set against, but that might just convince some of his own party that Muffle is right. They might just agree.'

The other three looked puzzled and Ernie Truscott whistled quietly through his teeth. This was something quite outside their experience: Standing Stillbury even considering the possibility of making an effort to think about causing something new to possibly happen.

'Where,' went on Henry Morgan, 'do we stand at the moment?'

Mr Clamp answered.

'No problem with planning. They could start building tomorrow. You saw that they seemed to like it and we just need their decision. There's been the usual grumble from the nearest end of Green Brook Estate, which is about 500 yards away – but I explained their options in t'community hall t'other night. Of course, they haven't a clue who it is yet – they'll like it even less when they know it's Germans. I haven't had any moans from Lower Middle Sniffley so far but there will be some when they've thought about it – the usual stuff about unwanted growth ruining the Town and all that.'

'The trouble with Lower Middle bloody Sniffley', went on Mr Clamp, rather matter-of-factly, 'is that they've all got bloody jobs and can't be bothered with them as hasn't.'

This was the one consistent problem area for Concrete Hardening. Lower Middle Sniffley had once been a completely separate little market town of undoubted charm, a certain local importance and considerable self-importance. It was the home of the professional classes and clerks of Concrete Hardening and it was the sort of place where the farmers from the surrounding countryside felt comfortable in the pubs on market days. Its resentment at being swallowed up by a growing big town was usually to be found fermenting somewhere or other. It was unforgiving about the brand new shopping centre a few miles away which had taken, so the shopkeepers claimed, trade that belonged to their shops. Their dreary little shops had mostly been in slow decline anyhow – but a new shopping centre is always an easy means of convincing oneself that the consequence of complacency and inertia is someone else's doing.

One local businessman had tried to liven up the dying centre of Lower Middle Sniffley by opening a sex shop. But his application for planning permission unleashed a row of Wagnerian proportions as the elders of the township solemnly declared that Lower Middle Sniffley would be the last place in the whole of Europe to have such premises in its midst. The thousand signatures on a petition in favour of the sex shop were dismissed as forgeries which could not possibly have been collected locally. In sense they were forgeries. A thousand or so people had indeed signed the petition but, this being Lower Middle Sniffley, not one had dared to use his own name and all had signed that of someone else.

The Town Council – an anomaly had allowed the retention of a town council, with parish powers only, once Concrete Hardening Council had become responsible for the real issues – had put forward its mini-mayor in a Radio Deepshire interview of such tragically biblical tone that tapes of the broadcast had found a sale in the local market, snapped up for their curiosity value and played to hoots of beery laughter at parties throughout Deepshire for years afterwards.

Whenever something new was planned, some ageing local pundit from this little backwater (usually someone who fondly remembered the 'good times' before everyone had indoor lavatories and Concrete Hardening got ambitious) could always be found to offer a juicy quote to the newest young reporter making a name on the Deepshire Planet or Radio Deepshire. It might be outrage about using good farmland for factories, envy about some new cinema that wasn't near enough to THEM or it might just be malice because Concrete Hardening was taking another firm step forward without giving a damn whether Lower Middle Sniffley objected or not. By the time of these events, it should be admitted, some Lower Middle Snifflies were getting resigned to their situation and contented themselves with the gesture of refusing to use the Concrete Hardening postcode on their correspondence.

For others, there was no time for more extensive gestures. They needed all the time they could get to indulge in the middle-class versions of state cadging at which Lower Middle Snifflies excelled no less than others, They revealed a mirror image of the roguish activities of the minority in some of the council estates in the less genteel parts of Concrete Hardening. Much of the gin drunk in Lower Middle Sniffley was paid for by un-needed but gratefully accepted family allowance payments. The place also had its fair share of disability allowances falling into the hands of equally grateful sufferers of undefined back ailments and a variety of nervous problems who nevertheless seemed to lead full and active lives.

Henry Morgan and the other two permitted themselves brief smiles. Mr Clamp was known to be rather straight talking when faced with people who had secure jobs opposing new factories for those who didn't. All towns, and Concrete Hardening was certainly no exception, bred a percentage of people whose greatest pleasure in life was to object to almost anything new – sometimes before they even knew exactly what it was. Sometimes it was just out of perversity; sometimes to foster local political ambitions; sometimes out of some past impotence in the face of officialdom which could leave a lifetime of cantankerous desire for revenge in its wake. And it was sometimes because they came from Lower Middle Sniffley, some of whose residents still did it automatically – even if the new development was several miles away, on the other side of Concrete Hardening.

But Mr Clamp was well used to dealing with this. Some of his younger staff found protest meetings in dusty village halls on Summer nights quite terrifying. But Mr Clamp had an effective combination of technique and conviction. He had found over the years that opposition arguments in these situations usually got more and more vapid as closing time approached at the local pub. He always had the patience to keep going, gently and courteously here, brusquely there, until the enemy slowly melted away leaving, usually, the vicar's wife and the local nutcase (there was always one, usually marked by wearing a woolly hat and bicycle clips throughout the evening and wanting to talk about some issue completely un-related to that under discussion) who would carry on until an indignant caretaker kicked them out. At this point Mr Clamp would feign intense disappointment and leave with what seemed the utmost reluctance – to be regarded as a friend for life of the flattered possessor of the woolly hat.

In referring to the vicar's wife and the local nutcase I should explain that these USUALLY constitute two separate people. But to avoid confusion I do concede that in one particular parish of Concrete Hardening they were, just a few years ago, one and the same.

The upshot of all this was that there would be no effective opposition in Concrete Hardening. They just needed Zugswang to decide if they were coming or not, preferably before the Company was faced with the unknown factor of how Standing Stillbury would mount a bid.

They all thought for a few minutes. Then Henry Morgan had an idea.

'Let's ask them over this coming weekend and take them out for a chat at the Castleton Races. I know it's a bit tin-pot but they probably never get to see the real side of places like Deepshire. They might just like it!'

The others, in turn, thought a little more. 'OK', reflected Brian Fichtl, 'I suppose we could try it. It has to be better than doing nothing.'

The others nodded and Henry Morgan picked up the telephone.

Chapter 8 – Slings and Arrows

But if Concrete Hardening had no effective opposition, Standing Stillbury did.

Whilst the politicians and those in the know had been chewing over the 'secret' plans for Zugswang, the word had at last become common currency on the North End Estate as well. This was the nearest residential part of Standing Stillbury to the site which Mr Muffle thought ideal for the factory.

It should be remembered that the North End Estate was populated by people who, mostly, didn't have too much time to philosophise about the effects upon their town of a new factory. They were generally busy trying to earn any sort of living at all, to feed and clothe small children, to get them to school on time or to scrape the money together for a holiday. But in a small minority of cases, they were desperately trying to avoid having a job, whilst skilfully exploiting the system of state benefits so as to minimise the need for one – or at least one which was admitted to.

This latter group could at least devote some time to considering the Zugswang development and decided that it didn't like it at all.

The local councillor was the same Fred Jones, Socialist, who had stood in the line to be presented at the previous week's royal visit. He had been accosted by a small delegation at the Furriers Arms public house (shortly to be re-named the Green Piece for reasons of political correctness, the decision following an aggressive public demonstration which had been led by a man wearing a real leather jacket) and persuaded to lead a public protest against the Zugswang plan. He was quite quickly persuaded because he had come to the Furriers Arms for a game of crown green bowls and wanted to get on with it during what remained of a pleasant, warm evening which went well with a pint or

two of the local mild beer. At least it had been local before
the brewery was bought out and quickly closed, production
being transferred to a distant city. The original name of the
beer had been retained for the nostalgic and for its commercial value. But the councillor had agreed to what the deputation had wanted, politely got rid of them and got on with his
bowls. He liked to joke that this was one activity in his life
in which he felt able to exhibit bias.

But Fred Jones was also pleased by the opportunity,
which he mulled over during the game. Local Councillors
thrive on popular protests and this one had all the elements
he needed. The factory could be presented as dirty and sure
to cause pollution. And it would be owned by foreigners –
and Germans ranked quite highly as foreigners on North
End Estate. He saw the chance to grab the credit for a campaign he could hardly lose: the Town Forum was against
Zugswang, the Council was divided and the Conservative
MP, God forbid but not just for the moment, was as good
as committed to being on his side. Delicious!

Plans were made quickly. The estate meeting hall was
booked for a public meeting on the following Monday at
7.30 pm, the day before the Policy and Resources Committee would take its decision. The Member of Parliament
was invited and the Council officials summoned to attend –
and in the day and age of this story council officials could
hardly avoid a summons to a public meeting. Mr Muffle, on
receiving Councillor Jones' telephone call had groaned inwardly but managed to send a thin smile down the
telephone line as he accepted the invitation.

The Councillor and the job-fearing dissenters quickly
drummed up support around the estate, aided by wild
rumours and the half-knowledge of the facts which they
imparted to local residents: common tactics when trying to
wreck a planned development.

Within a day or so the Germans were believed to be
importing all the workforce from Dusseldorf, paying half
the British rate for the job and insisting upon physical
exercises at 6.30 am, before the start of work each day, to
the tune of Deutschland Uber Alles. The fact that the latter
two claims would hardly matter if the workforce was

entirely German was lost in the torrent of speculation. Furthermore, the smoke from the chimney stacks would pour upon the North End Estate and local roads would be pounded day and night by heavy lorries supplying the factory and taking away its products.

Even the indifferent were quickly inflamed by the impending gross injustice of building such a factory on an industrial estate at their end of Standing Stillbury. 'There must', they all insisted, 'be somewhere else it could be built'. (Curiously, the same or similar sentiments had been voiced many years before when their own houses were built on what had been attractive meadowland. In that case the new houses had been said to be ruining the view enjoyed by the residents of some even older dwellings nearby.)

The meeting hall would be filled to bursting.

Chapter 9 – A Private Meeting

The protest swirled around North End Estate, and even spilled into other areas of Standing Stillbury. It was all too easy to find people who were passionately against anything new, even if they barely knew what it was. Standing Stillb'rians who had never contributed a positive idea to the life of their town in twenty years could be counted upon to react with outrage if someone else did.

But while this was happening, Member of Parliament Jack Fudge was 150 or so miles away in another room. The room was as dimly lit as the Mayor's Parlour at Standing Stillbury during the very first discussion about Zugswang weeks before. But it was rather more grand. The chairs were green-leather seated and backed, and each bore the distinctive crown and portcullis emblem of the House of Commons.

Mr Fudge was relaxed, his elbows on an oak table as he sipped from a large glass of brandy and listened with polite half-interest to the man across the table from him, Government Chief Whip Henry Nelson.

Henry Nelson was a small, wiry sort of man, in his late forties and only five feet four inches tall. But he had brains and an iron character and was clearly on his way up the rickety ladder of British politics. Whether this meant much any more, given the acute decline in Britain's importance in the world was debatable. At the height of empire, say in the early 1900s, entry to the Commons gave you at least a chorus-role on the world stage. A tub-thumping speech by a back-bencher might result in a dreadnaught pointing its twelve-inch guns in the direction of any malcontented little republic which failed to pay its bills to British traders or suchlike. By this time, getting into Westminster seemed a bit like the hollow success of women in becoming vicars when no-one very much went to church any more. But there were plenty who, as politicians, still found everything they sought in life – and Henry Nelson was one of them.

Beyond being Conservatives, he and Jack Fudge were not natural allies. They had few shared interests outside the House and they were on the thinly aimiable terms dictated by expediency. Government whips needed to humour their own people as best they could, for those occasions when their votes in the House became a matter of importance or even survival. They also needed to get a feel for how they were thinking. Back-benchers hoping for some small preferment tended to be pleasant to the whips. So, on a quiet day, and with the glasses of brandy, each was passively content with the company of the other.

They had been chatting about a number of issues which concerned the Government. Having lost its way hopelessly on both the domestic economy and the foreign relations of the United Kingdom, the latter was concerned to retrieve its reputation by promoting two new parliamentary bills. The purport of these was to increase the cost of dog licences and to define a whole new range of offences for which motorists could be stopped at random and brought to court at the whim of police officers who would be under pressure to fulfil quotas of such charges, daily.

There was a furtive hope amongst senior ministers that these measures would deflect some of the public outrage which had built up over a manifest failure to reduce or even stabilise the rate of car thefts, house burglaries and violent robberies committed in broad daylight against members of the public.

It was fair to say that there had been some disquiet amongst the governing party's members, all of whom owned cars and most of whom kept dogs. One junior, and very naive, Home Office Minister had actually suggested that the police should instead be made to fulfil quotas of arrests of people who stole cars, burgled houses or robbed the public violently in broad daylight.

This idea had caused two things: intense public interest and uproar amongst all ranks of the police. The public was very taken with an idea which sought to reduce real crime whilst making their motor cars less soft targets for both police and criminal activity. But the police, at senior level at any rate, screamed the idea down as quite imbecile, bearing in mind that those who committed the listed offences, when challenged, invariably drove off in the high-speed vehicles they had stolen, or, even worse, fired guns at their pursuers. Ordinary motorists, it was explained, were a much more natural subject for quotas as they always politely pulled over to the roadside and usually apologised when police officers roared up behind them with blue lights flashing and sirens wailing. They often apologised before they knew why they had been stopped.

But one senior police officer in the Home Counties had then gone a little too far. He had given a vitriolic television interview in which he personally insulted the minister responsible for the suggestion, describing him as a bird-brained make-weight at the Home Office. He had been suspended pending a disciplinary inquiry. Then, inevitably, he was declared unfit to appear, due to undefined stress-related illnesses, and retired early on a large pension. Senior police officers who offend in this sort of way seldom get to face disciplinary inquiries. In the inexplicably long months or even years before the enquiry happens, they always develop stress-related illnesses and have to be retired first.

The Government had been left feeling rather edgy after all this highly publicised fuss. So Henry Nelson and his colleagues in the Whip's Office were having private chats with people like Jack Fudge. Having daft ideas was one thing: being defeated over them in the House was another.

The purpose of the discussion would hardly have been apparent to the casual listener since only extreme doubt would provoke a whip into asking a fellow party-member outright about his voting intentions. If you did it too often the blighters might start to think they were supposed to have voting intentions.

So this conversation had merely drifted along pleasantly. No difficulty had emerged since, as usual, Jack Fudge appeared intent on voting with the Government, through thick and thin, still hoping in middle-age for the call to even junior ministerial office and a few brief years of minor importance before being jettisoned for a younger man in some future re-shuffle.

And that, though he didn't know it yet, was the second reason for this discussion.

It should be said that, despite their lack of ability to run a country terribly well, the Government, which term included the party whips, did not consist of stupid people. Some years before, a famous writer had referred to the Tory Party, in a newspaper article, as The Stupid Party. In consequence he brought down the wrath of the establishment upon his head (one was generally a bit more polite in those times) but had blandly explained in a subsequent article that he most emphatically did not mean that everyone in the Tory Party was stupid: merely that everyone who WAS stupid appeared to have joined it.

So there were actually plenty of people clever enough to form a government, even if they had been unlucky with the conduct of national affairs for the past year or so. And there was certainly no stupidity in asking someone of Jack Fudge's obvious limitations to join them.

They knew he wouldn't contribute much in the way of original thought. They knew he could get a bit ratty when under any sort of pressure. They knew that if some issue got a bit too hot on his own patch at Standing Stillbury, he would sometimes disappear from sight for a while and avoid any comment until it was all over – perhaps from a deep-seated fear of backing a wrong horse or having to criticise his own party's policies. His stance on the Zugswang factory was an exception to his normal rule, borne of a belief that he was well in tune with the mood of Standing Stillbury on any issue which threatened to engender progress.

But they also knew that, after many years in the House, he had a bit of a circle of like-minded fellow-members from the shires who shared an interest in preserving ancient army regiments from Treasury cuts and keeping up Britain's role in policing an empire reduced to little more than Gibraltar, the Falkland Islands and Hong Kong. So they had decided that the drift of events made it right to give him a year or two of junior office, whilst consolidating a small block of associated votes during the difficult period ahead. And there was the bonus, increasingly rare in the House, that he appeared to be personally honest and unencumbered with embarrassing directorships or desperately-needing-to-be-hidden consultancies.

Henry Nelson broached the subject gently.

'There is one other small thing . . .'

The slight change in his tone was quickly detected and Jack Fudge first felt apprehensive – had he done something wrong? Had some indiscretion or financial impropriety been alleged against him? He couldn't think what it might be, but desperately wondered, just the same. Whatever you did, it got back to the Whips sooner or later. It would be in that bloody book they kept.

But then it began to dawn that he might be hearing something to his advantage. He put the glass of brandy down and began to listen intently.

'The PM,', Henry Nelson had continued, 'has asked me to have a quiet word with you on another matter. You obviously know about the problem with young Miles Blockham?'

'Yes', the other replied, 'Who doesn't at the moment?' Remembering to whom he was talking, Jack Fudge firmly suppressed a slight smirk and forced his face to look stern and team-member-like.

Miles Blockham, Junior Minister at the Board of Trade, had almost certainly ruined a promising career by an unfortunate and ill-judged decision, taken in circumstances which were, admittedly, difficult.

The Government had, in public at least, assented grudgingly to a United Nations ban on the sale of arms to the brutal dictator of a small Central American republic which was routinely kidnapping its own people and disposing of them without trace in an effort to remain in unelected but profitable power. The dictator and his party had committed acts of genocide against the indigenous Indian population when their land had been needed for development, and violated almost every tenet of democracy and freedom which could be imagined.

The Government had known all about this but not cared

much, one way or the other. No vital British interest was threatened by the excesses and, indeed, it valued the healthy trade balance which Britain, as a favoured supplier, had been allowed by American acquiescence, to achieve in the tropical paradise.

But the state of affairs in the small republic, and the part played by British armaments in maintaining it, had been exposed thoroughly by a British television reporter whose inconvenient efforts in a documentary had shocked the nation one Thursday evening and eventually forced some response from both the UN and an embarrassed British Foreign Office.

But the first, immediate reaction had been for the television reporter to be branded a lying, left-wing agitator, very publicly, by several of the less cerebral members on the Government side of the House. That had been a terrible mistake. The reporter gleefully produced proof of several years exemplary membership of his local Conservative Party Association – whose members, displaying the honesty of purpose found in greater proportions the further one gets from Westminster, perversely supported him to a man. (Though they didn't have any section of the armaments industry in their particular constituency, it must be said.) He took full advantage of the controversy to remind the nation, in high moral tones during a television news interview, that mass murder and the abuse of power were wrong however friendly the wrong-doers had been with members of one's own government. 'The days of Lord Palmerston', he sternly reminded viewers, 'were long gone.'

Governments usually survive issues which merely induce moral outrage over events a long way off. Palmerston, in his day, had understood this very well indeed, generally deferring to large powers and trampling over smaller ones as the national interest dictated.

And some people even admire brutal, far-right regimes. But young Miles Blockham at the Board of Trade had then been faced with the problem of what exactly to do about lucrative arms exports to, shall we invent for the sake of delicacy, El Parador, upon which hundreds of jobs in finely-balanced parliamentary constituencies depended.

He might have got away with encouraging the Chairman of the main supplier company to keep the business, and the jobs, going – through a friendly third country which agreed to act as a warehouse on neutral ground. Quite a number of people secretly admire a decision of that sort. It can fall within a political twilight zone in which national interests are served by shameful means and the process kept from scrutiny and the troubles of all our consciences. But no other government department was told about this arrangement, naturally enough, and an investigation by an alert Customs and Excise official had uncovered the whole affair.

Even THAT might have been survivable if brazened out with hints of a bit of cynical swashbuckling to preserve British jobs. The public will often accept the dubious pursuit of British interests by someone who looks as if he can face down foreign politicians whilst shrouded in a Union Jack and waving two fingers. But Miles Blockham had then made his big, big mistake. The unfortunate company chairman was arrested and charged with illegal arms export offences. And the Junior Minister had taken the fateful decision to deny the fact of their past meetings and to suppress evidence which would have supported the defence, on the grounds of state security.

The sad and miserable reality was that his decision had been taken on the grounds of Miles Blockham's and the Government's security. But just before the astonished and disbelieving company head was to be sentenced at the end of an acrimonious trial, a senior official at the Board of Trade, whose conscience was larger than his ambition, had turned up at the defence solicitor's offices and spilled the whole story.

The defendant was immediately acquitted in a dramatic about-turn of the proceedings which dominated the national news media for several consecutive days. But the idea that a government minister could sit back and watch a man go to jail for doing the Government's bidding was beyond the tolerance of even the most cynical and jingoistic observer. The two sides of the House were enraged in a way which was both rare yet completely genuine.

The resignation of Miles Blockham was regarded as

inevitable in the face of mounting pressure from the honourable members, the public and the press. Sadly, the days when a minister might have resigned without these pressures, simply upon mature and honest reflection of the dreadfulness of his conduct, had long since passed in British politics. By this time, Critchel Down was a distant folk-memory, often quoted but seldom recalled in detail. Miles Blockham would cling, limpet-like, to the rock of office for a few days more and then be washed away by the next high tide of public and parliamentary wrath.

The civil servant who had saved the company chairman from jail would not face disciplinary action: an angry House would have exploded in the Government's face at that. But it would be a fair bet that, five years hence, he would be found languishing in the museum section of the National Heritage Office or looking after potato quotas at the Ministry of Agriculture, Fisheries and Food.

But all this meant, 'though it could not be said with absolute finality by the Chief Whip yet, that there would probably be a junior ministerial vacancy. 'We think, if it came to it', went on Henry Nelson, 'that you might be the man. We need a steady hand after all the fuss. Nothing official yet, of course. But if you ARE interested (a purely rhetorical courtesy) the approach will come from the PM through the usual channels.'

Grinning like a Welshman on a quango – he was by now half listening and half working out how to sound casual whilst dropping this news to his wife – Jack Fudge indicated his immediate assent to the suggestion. He privately thanked God that he had carefully avoided any strong public or private comment on the El Parador scandal, both at Westminster and back at Standing Stillbury. This was, as has been explained, his usual procedure on contentious issues, but he still thanked God. Then came the difficult part.

'There is another small matter', went on Henry Nelson, his voice now little more than a whisper. 'I gather you've actually taken a bit of a position over the question of Zugswang Components coming to Standing Stillbury. I'm sure it's the usual tedious exaggeration but expressions like 'over my dead body' seem to be floating up from your constituency association' – this all said with the friendliest of smiles.

The Member of Parliament paled slightly. What under-current had he missed. Who did Henry Nelson know in the Standing Stillbury Conservative Association? (Like all good whips, Henry Nelson knew many more people than most back-benchers realised. It was his business to do so).

'Well', countered Jack Fudge, trying desperately to pick up the flight of a ball which seemed to be hurtling towards his stumps, 'hardly THAT strong. It's really a matter for the local council – they do the planning and all that, of course.' He didn't take any runs but felt he might have blocked the googly just in front of middle.

Henry Nelson, in the guise of bowler and umpire com-bined, thought for a moment and raised no finger to the sky. Not out!

'Good, good,' he said, gently. 'You see the PM attaches great importance to the Zugswang project coming to the UK and we simply couldn't have one of us treating them as boarders to be repelled from the ship and all that.'

'Of course, not, of course not,' stuttered the Member for Standing Stillbury, slowly beginning to understand.

'In fact', went on the Chief Whip, the PM thinks it might be quite helpful if you actually came out in support of their coming to the Town. Of course, the chances are that they'll go for Concrete Hardening as most of them seem to do in your part of the World these days – so there won't really be much to lose.' There was a slight, almost imperceptible accent on 'much to lose' which sounded horribly as as if it related to junior ministerial office. 'It's just that' Henry Nelson went on lightly, 'we simply can't have them feeling unwelcome in case it sours the whole deal. You know how strangely sensitive they can be at times. You understand what I mean?'

Jack Fudge did. He had a vision of a smiling Prime Minister opening a splendid new German factory, taking credit for the enlightened government policies which had brought it all about and for the jobs and prosperity it would bring. He saw himself standing next to the PM as the Junior Minister at the Board of Trade. He suddenly saw the

Zugswang Company in a new and attractive light. Then he saw his next meeting with the Standing Stillbury Town Forum and with the local Conservative Association and felt a nervous twinge in the pit of his stomach.

But the feeling lasted little more than a second. 'Yes,' he replied decisively, 'I understand perfectly'.

Henry Nelson almost beamed. The deal was done. Then he stuck the knife in, so smoothly that it could hardly be felt at first. 'And the PM thinks,' he breathed, 'that it might help if you could use your good offices to make sure the Council makes welcoming noises as well – not to get them to Standing Stillbury, I do stress, just to make them feel wanted.'

As this request sank in, Jack Fudge's agreement was distorted by alarm at the discomfort of such a task so as to emerge as a slight choking noise. But Henry Nelson, taking acquiescence for granted was already leaving the room. A distant bell sounded but didn't penetrate Jack Fudge's brain for some seconds. Then he jumped up with a start. It was the division bell – time to vote on the first reading of the Dog Licence Bill. He rushed off not wanting to be late for THAT after a sounding-out for junior ministerial office.

Chapter 10 – A Day at the Races

Herr Grossemann and Herr Pfennig had accepted the invitation to more discussions combined with a visit to the Castleton Races. This was a pleasant surprise. It arose from the unspoken philosophy of Concrete Hardening: if you asked for what you wanted, you sometimes got it. This was in stark contrast to the philosophy of Standing Stillbury, evolved and matured over many centuries: if anybody thought of a new idea for the Town, everybody else felt morally obliged to come up with fifty reasons why it wouldn't work. Both towns had their share of people like this, of course. It was just that in Standing Stillbury they were often the ones who ran the place.

Castleton, half way between Standing Stillbury and the Lower Middle Sniffley side of Concrete Hardening, was hardly a racecourse at all. It was simply a rough, tufty grass track with a number of brushwood jumps. It ran for about three miles through farm fields adjoining the River Septon, a few miles downstream of the County Town.

But the Castleton Races, an annual event, always on the same bank holiday Monday, was beloved by large numbers of people from all parts of Deepshire's two main towns and the surrounding country districts. It was one of THE events in the social calendar.

The racing was not of the kind found at silky-smooth Ascot where even the bookies had suits which almost fit, or even at far northern Doncaster where they didn't. This was country racing, or point-to point, where the riders were all amateurs and where, despite the vagaries of Jockey Club officialdom, all the races seemed to start efficiently and first time. The horses could not be trained racers – they had to be hunters which went out regularly with the hounds. This was a matter of increasing difficulty amidst the hateful sub-politics of the time, when foxes were that year's perceived victims, fish in the rivers would be the next (though the voting power of the country's huge fishing lobby would make that a much tougher issue) and, who knows, there was probably a vegetable liberation front being formed for the year after that. The common thread which linked all crusades of this kind was the utter certainty of moral rightness enjoyed by their adherents and, in extreme cases, the deeply held belief that killing people was justified to save animals or, in the event of a VLF really being formed, Jerusalem Artichokes.

But the Castleton Races still survived and it would have been a bold animal rightist who tried to disrupt them. He would have had to face five or six thousand enthusiastic supporters, sprinkled with plenty of muscular, ruddy-faced farmers and their men – the latter aided by lager-soaked teenage townies who would have loved the opportunity to deal out some violence with a rare public approbation. And besides, the deep moral certainty of the animal rightists was usually at its most morally certain deep in the night, when their furtive crimes of protest could not be witnessed by anyone who might recognise them. It tended to evaporate in front of witnesses in daytime.

The long course through the fields was much tougher than would be the case in high-class racing. The standard of the competitors was much more varied as well. Some of the horses at Castleton look fit for the knacker's yard and the glue factory after just a couple of fences – and the same goes for some of the riders. Others get around the three miles of track pretty well. A few even look as if they are fading and having almost to climb over the last fence or so – a strange sight. But some come in strongly to raucous cheers from their backers, looking as if they could go round again. The irritating thing is that you can never tell the jumpers and stayers from the faders and climbers by looking at them in the oval parade ring beforehand. Judging horses by their looks is even harder than judging men by the same means.

But the quality of the racing and the sophistication of the course were not the reasons for bringing the Managing Director and the Finance Director of Zugswang Components for a day's outing. No-one very much came to

Castleton for those things. One came to Castleton to enjoy
a bit of shire-county life and perhaps to observe others
doing the same. In this specific case, there was also the hope
of bringing about a business deal. The leaders of Concrete
Hardening Council had become even more convinced for
thinking about it that their guests might appreciate the day.
Castleton Races were not at the top or even the middle-level
of smartness as race meetings went. Few foreign visitors
ever got there. This was a bit of real England.

The Zugswang party was collected from Concrete Hardening Central Station early in the day and taken to the
nearby Concrete Hardening Hotel where the Council had
reserved rooms for them. After some time to settle in, they
were met in the foyer by Henry Morgan, Brian Fichtl and
Ernie Truscott to be driven, in a hired Renault Espace, the
few miles to Castleton.

The Germans seemed relaxed and happy. They chatted
with their hosts about this and that and enjoyed the picture
of English countryside which passed the Espace's windows.
So there was no annoyance when, still on one of Deepshire's main A-roads, they were stuck for several miles
behind a grindingly slow farm tractor which appeared to
carry no vehicle registration-plate of any kind. This was a
hazard of driving throughout Deepshire, especially as the
sugar-beet season set in at the beginning of Winter.

The chauffeur, detecting the relaxed mood of his passengers, took no unnecessary risk to overtake and finally
gained speed when the tractor turned into a side road. He
reflected upon his own long-felt desire, so far suppressed, to
pull in front of a farm tractor and reduce his own speed to
precisely two miles per hour less than its driver wanted to
go – for at least ten miles.

As a matter of fact, the long-promised day would eventually come when this particular A-road would be up-graded
to a dual-carriageway. There would be great anguish at the
National Farmers Union over the sudden freedom of motorists to shoot effortlessly past lumbering farm vehicles with
their manure-strewn trailers.

Emergency meetings would be held, jointly with the
Caravan Club of Great Britain, whose members would

experience a similar loss of power to thwart the motorist and, in consequence, bouts of stress and anxiety. The more impetuous, younger members would propose meeting the challenge by driving two-abreast, to keep things as they had been, but in the end they'd all have to swallow it and find a new hobby.

As the Espace approached Castleton, the junctions were watched over by police officers who shared the available roadspace fairly amongst the traffic arriving from different directions. Such were Deepshire and the Castleton Races that, year after year, the same policemen would be seen at the same road junctions. It was a well-organised routine.

As they got closer to the course, the traffic fell into a slowly moving queue for a few minutes and then divided into two lanes. Those wanting the best parking spaces, inside the vast circuit around the river-plain chose the left lane. Those willing to walk a bit further went right and paid less. The Concrete Hardening party naturally went into the left lane.

Strictly speaking, the Jockey Club never used to allow spectators to be charged at point-to-point racing – but as racing cannot function without income, the money taken for parking is effectively the admission charge. But the money-bagged collectors, near the bottom of a long and strictly graded hierarchy of race officials, seem to charge a pound even if you walk to the event these days. Perhaps the rules have changed.

Inside the course, long before the first race at 2.0 pm, the assorted society of Deepshire was arriving. They came in all kinds of vehicles from Rolls Royces to Reliant Robins. With the exception of one group, there was no set form of dress for Castleton Races – so the few people who conspicuously did dress for the races, in smart tweedy suits with dark brown trilbys and highly polished brown shoes, looked odd and incongruous.

Some of the racegoers opened car boots, hauled out picnic hampers, poured wine, chatted happily, greeted old friends, made new ones, poured more wine. Relatives were treated, business deals cemented, dogs walked and scream-

ing, shrieking children good naturedly indulged. Others just
lay around on the grassy bank which rose above the course
at its western end. They enjoyed picnics and drank beer –
straight from the cans in most un-Deepshire fashion.

Some of the more energetic had developed the habit of
strolling around the whole of the circuit in the hour or so
before racing started, returning with an especially good
appetite and a thirst.

Amongst the various picnics and entertainments, some,
usually at the back of a newish Range Rover or something
similar, stood out in their magnificence. The wine would be
champagne. That and heavy measures of spirits would be
jovially offered to passing friends and acquaintances – of
whom large numbers always emerged from the crowd,
faces reddening, voices heightening in loudness and pitch as
the day wore on. One or two of next year's bankruptcies
were often to be found amongst the donors of this largesse.
When that happened, few friends emerged from the crowd
any more. The old money at Castleton Races arrived in
battered Land Rovers and enjoyed itself just as much, but a
shade more quietly.

The uniformed driver, who came with the Renault
quickly chose a good vantage point amongst all the jollity,
pulled out collapsible chairs and made his charges comfortable. Food and drink followed and a pleasant glow soon
descended upon the proceedings, the more so since the day
was blessed with dry, warm weather. The guests were particularly intrigued to be offered Deepshire Blue, a pungent
local cheese with prominent veins throughout its waxy
orange-coloured substance which settled nicely on the
stomach with bread and a glass of decent Mosel – chosen
diplomatically in preference to Sancerre.

The Germans could hardly conceal their fascination with
the variety of human shapes and types with which they
were surrounded. The races attracted the old, the young,
the fat, the thin, the rich and the poor. The cost of entry to
Castleton Races barred no-one who really wanted to be
there. There was even an entire birthday party which had
arrived by coach, already well enlivened by beer. The party
passed through the parked vehicles in a shrieking, scream-

img, inelegant and un-musical conga. No-one seemed to mind in the least.

For some, racing seemed not to feature in the proceedings at all. They made rapidly for the beer tent and wouldn't emerge until the end of the day when the workmen started to take it down and they had to get out. Every race meeting in the world seems to attract this strange breed whose motivation is unclear. They have to pay to get into the course but would be outraged if asked to pay for admission to their local pub on days when there is no racing. Castleton, like other racecourses, also harboured that now endangered British species, the unsavoury character. They are not easily spotted by the unpracticed eye. There is just something about their manner of dress and slight lack of a shave which marks them out. They don't seem to have any particular reason for being at the course, though recognition of the species causes an involuntary movement of the hand to check that one's wallet is still in place. They are never seen arriving or leaving but do place a bet from time to time. The fearful certainty of attracting unsavoury characters is often given as a reason by worried middle-class objectors to planning applications for betting shops in their neighbourhood. This seems a pity as the species might eventually be sanitised out of our national life and no longer available for study of its fragile life-style. People who fret about the extinction of the Large Blue Butterfly never give a damn about the British Unsavoury Character.

The beer tent, though, was most heavily populated by the 'nominally 18' to 25-year-old group, whose members actually seemed to be as young as 12. This was where the one thing approximating to an agreed correct form of dress was found in large numbers. Swarms of boys and girls (or gels) congregated, dressed alike in waxed green jackets, green wellington boots and brown trilbys, more uniform, the males at least, than the Prussian Guard. They all, with great gusto, drank large quantities of warm and grossly over-priced beer from pint plastic beakers. The gels, wore the same basic and rigidly defined uniform as the boys, but permitted themselves silken scarves of distinctive colours and patterns. This, clearly, was so that each of the boys would take the right one home at the end of the day's cavorting and drinking. As the day wore on, this group, getting steadily more drunk, tended to spill out of the tent in order to perform boisterous antics for the benefit of the more reserved racegoers. They were ignored as far as was possible.

In the distance, at the far end of the site, the screams and yells of small children could just be heard as they enjoyed a travelling funfair which the organisers, the South Deepshire Hunt, always allowed on the site. Nearer at hand stalls were being set up by the bookmakers. They were all, fifteen or so, angelic-looking pictures of life's finer qualities who came from places like Salford or Rochdale. They wore battered hats and leather-elbowed jackets, creased like their worry-furrowed faces. Later that day they would return furtively to their home towns in cars carefully chosen for inconspicuous shabbiness, clutching leather satchels of Deepshire money gained by manipulation of the most mean and ungenerous odds. But since, for the majority of the crowd, the racing was almost incidental to the day, there were seldom any great complaints. You didn't expect to come out ahead on the betting and if, occasionally, it happened, you took that as a bonus on a pleasant day out.

There were usually better terms to be had when a tote operated, but the tote didn't always appear and there wasn't one on this day. There would sometimes be an elderly lady, perhaps at the races for the first time, who would grumble about not being able to place a 50p bet: the minimum was £1. But that was about it.

But when the racing started, there were some people, just a few, who took it very seriously. These were people who dressed quietly and stayed pretty sober. They seemed to look very closely indeed at the horses as they were led around the parade ring, and then to draw some sort of conclusion from what they had seen. They often held back from the crowds jostling around the bookies' stalls, waiting for the odds on some fancied animal to shift a little in favour of the punter. When that happened, two or three hands would thrust forward, offering bundles of creased five or ten pound notes, the name of the horse shouted above the burble of the mob. The bookie would repeat the name and the amount to be won for a winning bet, handing out a cardboard betting ticket as his writer scribbled the details in the big book which gives the trade its name.

After a few bets like this, the bookie would get nervous and decline any more – 'no more for now, that's it thank you' – until he had shifted the odds back a little in his own favour. As soon as he did this the big bets would quickly dry up.

Sometimes, the people who had placed the large bets in such knowing fashion appeared to win. They won in about the same proportion as the once-a-year punters who barely knew one end of a horse from another.

The German guests happily accepted the suggestion that they join the fun. They read through the race card. The card always lists many more horses for each race than arrive on the day. Presumably some get lost or are stolen in transit. There is an old joke about an Irishman towing an empty horse box and getting stopped by the police. They ask him what he is about and he explains that he is taking the non-runners to Cheltenham. So, at Castleton, you have to listen carefully to the tannoy as the names of the horses which will run are listed by a metallic sounding voice. (I used to think this was the effect of the tannoy until I met the man who actually does the announcing). You put a tick on the race card against the name of each announced runner and usually have a dozen or more from which to choose.

Herr Grossemann, beginning to reveal a small sense of humour, noticed that the first race had been entered by 'Panzer', owned by a local farmer who also had a sense of humour – since 'Panzer' was not, in fact, fast enough to race through the low countries or anywhere else. He bet on it. The joke was enjoyed and expanded upon when Brian Fichtl, grinning, felt able to return the compliment and backed 'Spitfire', which was, as it happened, rather poor in the air and fell at the second fence. A third horse added to the excitement by shedding its rider and jumping into the river. This happened occasionally and the horse would be coaxed out of the water, usually quite un-damaged, a hundred yards or so downstream. There would be irritation expressed by nearby anglers who were float-fishing for large but wholly inedible chub, their size 8 hooks baited with marble-sized balls of cheddar cheese – but the water, aided by the gentle current, would quickly enough return to a state of calm and clarity and the chub would soon drift back to be tempted by the bait.

Everyone was now laughing or talking and there didn't seem to be any ice left to break. Even the unbelievably abysmal and primitive lavatory facilities were examined with good humour by Herr Grossemann. They consisted, for the men at least, of an area screened from public view by sheets of canvas mounted on poles, behind which one pee'd into a trough consisting of long sheets of corrugated iron bent into a sort of 'V' shape – when viewed from either end at least. The overlapping sheets of corrugated iron sloped, gradually descending to their lowest point, at which place the contents, by then a miniature torrent, poured into a hole in the ground to soak away. Herr Grossemann said he believed it had been just the same on the Russian front where his brother had served during the War.

The crowd continued to grow as a steady line of late-comers drove into the fields. The race officials, stern-looking men in long, pale-coloured mackintoshes, always with hats, looked important on their elevated platforms from which they peered through binoculars at distant but unspecified events. The policemen still looked relaxed as they strolled amongst the people. It would only get difficult at the end of the day when one or two of the younger drinkers would get a bit stroppy and need forceful persuasion to go home without first biffing some passing elderly gent.

But there was a pause in the eating and talking. Herr Pfennig glanced at his Chairman who nodded imperceptibly. He looked at Henry Morgan.

'The site could be OK for us. It is possible. But if we decided on Concrete Hardening, we would take at least two years to get into full production. We would need to defer half of the payment for the land until the end of that time – and we would need help with recruitment since we don't know your locals.'

Henry Morgan glanced at his two councillors – who barely reacted at all since they had already given him carte blanche and had heard nothing to dismay them.

'I think we could fix that. And we could do your recruitment from inside our own offices. The applicants wouldn't even need to know exactly who you are until you decide to go public.'

The Germans nodded. They didn't say anything very much and their hosts pointedly didn't press them. Since no-one seemed in a hurry to go, they had some more to eat and to drink and decided on their bets for the sixth race.

Chapter 11 – A Public Meeting

Mr Muffle, The Mayor and Jack Fudge didn't have such a pleasant day, though each came out of it better than he had expected.

On the evening of the Castleton race meeting, quite unaware of the outing which had been arranged for the Zugswang directors, they arrived at the dusty and un-cared-for community hall in the middle of North End Estate. The hall was cheaply constructed with wood panels and a felt-covered roof and the fact that it hadn't been set on fire years before was an eloquent testament to the fact that miracles were still possible. It sat amongst a few miserable local shops from which tired shopkeepers sold cigarettes and over-priced cans of beer to the strutting under-aged, keeping a careful eye open as they did so for the rare visit of a policeman. Their shop-fronts were all covered with heavy, depressing metal grilles once they had closed for the evening, a necessary precaution against the apprentice criminals of the area.

Some of the hall's windows had been broken and were boarded with plywood. In the lavatories, most of the copper pipework had been pulled loose from its supporting brackets by local children. When, occasionally, someone had a moan about this to the parents, the response would be flat denial of the possibility, outright abuse or a dismissive 'Shouldn't of made it so stoopid-like.' The idea of paying for the damage and rebuking the children never seemed to be remotely under consideration. In similar fashion, the Council or, as often, the mysterious 'they' took the blame for the heaps of sweet-wrappings, fish and chip papers, cigarette packets and other litter strewn around the hall and the shops. The idea that the litter could only have been dropped by local residents and their children was beyond contemplation. 'They' would always be blamed until it finally dawned upon some local Isaac Newton that Standing Stillbury didn't have organised gangs of roving litter-droppers who came round late each night to do their dirty work. The litter was home-made.

The desolate aspect of the environs was the result of activity by gangs of youths who congregated nearby most Summer evenings, devising new limits to which they could push public tolerance of their drinking, screaming, fighting, urinating, stone throwing, wall defacing, window smashing and, occasionally, copulating. Between certain hours, people who were not of their ilk simply avoided the place unless they had to get into the hall for some function. In that event they risked verbal abuse at best and being spat upon or even assaulted on a bad night. The police were often criticised for failing to take action. They were always 'aware of the problem' and 'had the matter in hand'. They had been saying this for years, though doing sod-all about it, secretly cursing the parents who seemed indifferent to the miseries inflicted by their offspring. The problem, in part, was that thirty years before, the parents of the worst offenders had been the ones congregating around the hall.

Once the teenagers reached 15 or 16 and could swagger un-challenged into a number of the local pubs, they would graduate to evenings of high-gravity lager consumption, enlivened by homeward journeys during which illuminated traffic bollards would be randomly kicked over to raucous shrieks of drunken glee. Instead of jumping heavily on this new sport, the whole apparatus of the law from constable to courtroom, had reacted with such lassitude as to render it no more than a minor transgression, thus breeding an attitude of mind which made more serious crime conceivable to the perpetrators. Indeed, the Council had reacted by replacing the bollards with cheap plastic shells which could easily be replaced and thus let another defence-line of civilised life be overrun without so much as a squawk. They should, of course, have made every fifth or sixth one from cast iron so that, just occasionally, an offender might have broken a leg.

This evening, though, there would be catcalls and foul language drifting in through the open windows, but not from too close by. The youths knew instinctively that the limits of tolerance were less when there were large numbers of beer-bellied adult males present.

Mr Muffle accompanied the Mayor who had made the official car available. They expected to hear some angry views about new factories.

The community hall and the small shops were surrounded by rows of almost identical three-bedroomed houses, unmistakably of council stock. Generations of idle or unimaginative council architects had been unwilling or unable to design council houses with any sort of separate identity. They would never be mistaken for privately-owned houses, even private houses which had cost less to build: they were unmistakably council houses and all looked much the same. It was the sort of estate in which you had to know the number of the house you were visiting. No other feature save perhaps the colour of the curtains marked one dwelling from another. The same sort of architects had even built small clusters of these houses, from the same pattern book it seemed, on the most unsuitable sites in the surrounding rural villages. There, they stood out even more ridiculously, not a single concession having been made to local variations in style or material. They were Standing Stillbury Council Houses and that was that.

The hall itself was thronged by two or three hundred people who cheered or booed as the councillors and officials of various views arrived. The Member of Parliament actually received a few cheers. For this to happen in the North End Estate was akin to a cannibal being welcomed at a vegetarian restaurant. However, his welcome appeared to give him no pleasure at all.

Several people marched up and down the pavement carrying placards on the end of wooden poles. They bore the words 'Say No To The FACTORY.' Mr Muffle, arriving to loud boos, harboured the thought that the local green party kept stocks of these placards carrying the pre-printed message 'Say No To The' with a space for the final word to be added as soon as the identity of any new project of any kind could be discovered. Certainly the placards seemed very uniform in appearance, except for the word

'FACTORY', which had obviously been written by hand, with a black felt-marker. They were remarkably like those which had appeared from time to time elsewhere in the Town, carried in protest against other new ideas. Standing Stillbury was a town with a good record of saying 'no' to 'the', whatever the 'the' might be.

And there was an odd aspect to this hatred of novelty. Provided that you succeeded in creating something new in Standing Stillbury, in the teeth of all the usual opposition and warnings of disaster, the new thing, whatever it was, only had to survive for about twenty years for the process to be reversed. At that point, and it always took about twenty years plus or minus one or two, any proposal to REMOVE whatever it was, would arouse the most frantic protests and even street marches and public demonstrations. The feeling would be that the heritage of the Town was under serious threat from unfeeling vandals.

As Mr Muffle and the Mayor entered the hall, Mr Horrocks, the Chauffeur, remained resolutely in the driver's seat of the Daimler, determined that his hub-caps should all remain in place. He was out of date in his thinking. By this time it was the wheels themselves and even the entire car which needed watching. But of course, keeping the hub-caps secure meant that the wheels or the car couldn't be removed either so he remained oblivious to the expansion of his imagined danger.

Inside the hall, rows of plastic stacking chairs, the ones used for the weekly bingo-session, had been brought out from the storeroom and placed so as to face the raised stage at one end of the room. On the stage was a long table so arranged that the platform party could face the crowd. To one side, a large map of Standing Stillbury had been pinned to the wall. The North End Housing Estate and the nearby Industrial Estate of the same name were both identified by bold red edging.

Mr Muffle was even more subdued than usual. He knew he was in for a difficult time. But he couldn't understand why the loudest opponent of his plans, Jack Fudge, seemed in no better spirit. That puzzled him. It also puzzled the Mayor, Fred Meadows, who had felt obliged to appear as well, still uncertain of his own position and hoping to know more after this evening. The meeting was to be chaired by Councillor Fred Jones, charged-up with the wrath of the righteous and counting upon the support of a baying mob of his very own local electors.

The crowd pushed and shoved its way through the narrow doorway to grab the seats. One of their number triumphantly entered with a video camera, complete with tripod, and announced his intention of recording the proceedings, so that any promises from the platform might be put beyond future dispute or quibble. This species quite often appears at public meetings these days, smirking with self importance and brandishing his recorder in phallic fashion, just waiting for a later chance to prove some reported remark either right or wrong depending upon the circumstances. The video-recorder is usually funded by some sort of community arts project. Those on the platform cheerfully smiled their agreement, 'though it had not exactly been asked for, keeping their real thoughts to themselves, behind clenched teeth.

The hall was soon packed with around three hundred people. Two hundred and fifty of them were seated, with the remainder standing at the back, obscuring a notice which, for safety reasons, limited the number in the hall to two hundred for any event. Reporters from the Deepshire Planet and Radio Deepshire had squeezed themselves into the gangway, poised with shorthand notebook and tape-recorder to catch all the details of what, in media-speak, was to be headlined, 'FACTORY ROW ERUPTS'.

As the unwilling visitors took their seats, to theatrical hisses and catcalls, they all noticed the figure of Tommy 'Trotsky' Turner in the middle of the second row. He frowned from behind a heavy black moustache which framed the lower part of his face, above a thick, fawn-coloured woollen cardigan. Several buttons were missing from the cardigan. Those which remained appeared not to have been pushed through the right buttonholes, giving the garment a strangely warped appearance. Possessing no suit, 'Trotsky' Turner regarded the cardigan as his Sunday best and had recently attended a wedding in it. He had been oblivious to the frantic efforts of the bride's mother to keep him out of as many photographs as possible.

He had the very leftist political views implied by his nickname though he couldn't have defined Trotskyism to save his life – and neither was he very clear about who Trotsky had been. He had never gained a seat on the Council, despite several attempts, even from the North End Ward – but had plenty of the shallow political support to be found in the bar-rooms of public houses in the area. He cast a loud and sometimes foul-mouthed pall over the proceedings of any meeting he attended. He was no friend of Councillor Fred Jones or any of the others on the platform. He hadn't been able to work for several years due to back trouble but felt that his regular hand-outs from the tax-payer were well justified as making possible his full contribution to local political life. Every other council estate the length of England seems to spawn one of this kind. It seems like a law of nature. In middle-class areas the equivalent is usually a Liberal called Jeremy or Nigel, who doesn't swear and rides a bike with a wicker basket attached to the handlebars.

Fred Jones called for quiet and opened the meeting. He introduced his guests – to his left, Mr Muffle, the Town Clerk and the man who wanted Zugswang in the Town; Mr Meadows, the Mayor, to his right, who had come with an open mind; Member of Parliament Jack Fudge even further right. The Councillor explained with some relish that Jack Fudge was on record as saying that Zugswang would come to Standing Stillbury over his dead body. The statement set off wild cheering. This was not the part of town where Jack Fudge got most of his votes (though several in the area did secretly vote for him out of despair at the alternatives) and the cheering was perhaps a mixture of gratitude for his perceived view of the issue and at the prospect of seeing his dead body.

The Mayor was invited to speak first, to outline the facts of the case, the nature of the Company, the precise boundaries of the site and so on. Whilst lacking Mr Muffle's brains, the Mayor was very good at this sort of thing. He had already decided upon his strategy to meet one particular problem.

The problem was Trotsky Turner whose plan of attack had little variety.

The Mayor began. 'The news about Zug . . .'

The loud, grating voice of a half-risen figure interrupted from the middle of the second row. 'C-R-A-P! You can take the bloody lot of them somewhere else!'

The Mayor exhuded smiling politeness and, rather surprisingly, sat down immediately, leaving the floor to the speaker whose intervention had generated a frenzy of cheering and applause around the room. The crowd loved to see some of 'them' getting, as they saw it, stuffed in this fashion. For a few seconds Trotsky acknowledged the ecstatic reaction to his rudeness, beaming with self-satisfaction and nodding to individuals he recognised here and there.

But since he actually had little of substance to say, he then found himself in some difficulty. The crowd very slowly quietened, the Mayor was seated, still smiling, and the interruptor was standing amidst an audience which clearly expected him to continue. Since his style of contribution depended upon the official speaker getting angry and exchanging insults at increasing levels on the Bolsover Scale, he could only fling a few more inanities and sit down.

The Mayor rose once more . . .

'The news about Zugswang was originally picked up when rumours started to go around about a large German company which wanted to make car comp . . .'

'*BOLLOCKS* you bloody idiot', boomed the voice from the second row. The Mayor smiled sweetly again and sat down, deferring to this new interruption which elicited more cheers and yells. But, once again, Trotsky had to fall silent after a few more idiocies, mostly quite unrelated to the matter in hand.

The Mayor rose again, 'They wanted to make car components for the British market and thought that somewhere in Deepshire would be the right place to . . .'

The voice came again. 'It bloody wouldn't you damn fool – make 'em take it to soddin' Liverpool . . .'

This time there were fewer cheers and a distinct feeling that some of the audience wanted to hear what the Mayor was trying to say. One or two of the brighter ones smiled as they began to see what was happening. Trotsky remained oblivious the direction in which he was being steered so delicately by the Mayor.

The Mayor pressed on, ready to finish the first skirmish of the night. 'Deepshire was seen as the right place because it has a pleasant environment and . . . '*DONT BE SO F----G STUPID*' came the rasping voice once more, suddenly, from row 2.

This time, the interruption was greeted with silence – the repetitiveness of the event, the Mayor's refusal to be drawn into crowd entertainment with Trotsky and the crudeness of the language being too much even for an audience which was hostile to the factory project. A young woman at the back, holding a damp-looking, runny-nosed baby, shrieked 'Why don't you bleedin' shut it – we can't 'ear what 'e's sayin'!'

The weight of feeling and emotion at a meeting of this kind can hang on a thread. The woman had never made a public comment in her life before. But her natural timing was perfect. Her interjection was greeted by thunderous cheering, and shouts of approval and foot-banging. The hero of just minutes earlier was suddenly the villain. Jack Fudge glanced across at Fred Meadows with something approaching admiration – one professional appreciating some unexpected good work from another.

Precisely as the Mayor had calculated, the reaction of the now enraged Trotsky was to leap up, hurl some more obscenities, this time at the crowd, and noisily stamp out, followed by calls of abuse directed at the retreating back of the fawn cardigan . . . 'noisy barsted . . . drunken sod . . . no f---g loss at all . . .' and so on. He would head for the Black Bull Inn, where the sawdust on the floor was sometimes the previous night's furniture. At 6ft 2ins and fifteen stone, much of it perched over his thick leather trouser-belt, Trotsky Turner usually got a good hearing at the Black Bull.

The Mayor was now faced by a silence more complete and polite than if Trotsky hadn't appeared at all, a natural pendulum effect as sentiment swung from one extreme to the other. So he continued to describe how the factory might fit into the North End Industrial Estate and, fearing the worst from the Member of Parliament, went out of his way to be fair to Mr Muffle by explaining the possible advantages. Despite his misgivings, he didn't intend to abandon his Town Clerk to a total shredding by Jack Fudge. Some of those present actually began to listen and, even more surprisingly, to hear what he was saying.

But Jack Fudge had been sitting through most of this in unusual silence, squirming occasionally and looking as if he would rather have been somewhere else. In fact he had decided that he had made a rare tactical mistake and should have been somewhere else, perhaps pleading Parliamentary business or even illness.

But now, Fred Jones, almost gloating, called upon him to speak and awaited the demolition of the plans for Zugswang from this unlikely political ally.

But it didn't quite go to plan.

Despite his discomfiture, Jack Fudge remained an accomplished public performer. So his intention was not immediately apparent.

He put on his most relaxed, languid voice which drifted in waves, gently across the hall.

'. . . great pleasure to have been asked to come tonight . . .'

(Mutters at the back of 'Tory prat'. 'Sssssssh' from others.)

'. . . always believed that local residents should have their say in these matters . . .'

(Whisper of 'He didn't say that about his brother's new bloody golf course . . .')

'. . . and any Member of Parliament worth his salt will come along and listen to what . . .'

(More whispers, louder now, 'Get f——ing on with it!')

'But it isn't simple to come to a decision when there are jobs at stake and no community can afford to turn its nose up at jobs unless the disadvantages are very great indeed – and I am here to see that you don't suffer great disadvantages . . .'

(Mr Muffle's eyebrows were raised just a fraction. This was a little more subtle than he had come to expect from

Jack Fudge.)

'So I have looked very closely at the idea of putting this factory here. As you know, my first thought, and it may still be right, was that you simply wouldn't want it. I was, on very fine balance, against it.'

('On fine balance!?' Mr Muffle repeated to himself, inaudibly, his eyebrows arching a little more.)

'But it turns out that there wouldn't be any pollution with the new technology Zugswang uses – and the height of the factory could actually be controlled by the planners at the Town Hall' – this last said with an almost friendly nod to Mr Muffle.

'So, whilst I haven't come here to dictate to you, and indeed, have no power at all to do so, my advice would be to think quite seriously about this and really consider what those jobs might do for the area. We could even see if they are willing to guarantee some to people in this estate.'

At this comment a few faces in the now silent audience fell visibly – but a number more brightened and looked interested. Councillor Fred Jones, who had detected the change of tack by the MP a little later than Mr Muffle, was by now red-faced and angry-looking, convinced he had been stabbed in the back for party political spite. Jack Fudge would normally have enjoyed doing that. But this time, he hadn't. The Councillor's predicament was the worse for his having spent the previous few days boasting around the estate about how he had lined-up the Tory MP to support him. 'Eating out of my hand' was one expression he suddenly recalled using. He began to choke a little, inwardly.

But the Member of Parliament carefully saved some of the Councillor's face with a creamy-smooth finish. This was not the moment to be creating enmity.

'Of course, Councillor Jones brought me along tonight, generously putting party differences aside, so that I could join him in supporting your wishes – and I know we both want the best outcome for North End Estate. We (with some stress on this word) both want you (with some stress on that word) to take a sensible decision and get the best out of the situation for North End. But I don't think this is something for a hasty decision.'

Now all classes of society in Standing Stillbury were amenable to the idea that things were not for hasty decisions. Councillor Jones was astonished to find himself sharing, by an embracing gesture of the MP's hand, a mild ripple of applause at these comments.

A question was shouted. 'Aren't they all bloody Germans?'

Standing Stillbury saw few foreigners outside the annual festival of song in the Castle grounds – and they mostly seemed to come from Finland or countries which had been on our side in the late war.

But Jack Fudge stayed on his feet and answered the question.

'It is a German company, I realise,' he replied, gently, 'and I do understand the real and genuine difficulties that poses for some people', this accompanied by a condescending nod to one or two older men with beerily red noses and British Legion lapel badges, 'but all that was a long time ago after all – and as I understand it, there would only be one or two Germans running it – the rest would be taken on here and trained.'

'And, (in a brief and rare moment of mildly humorous inspiration) I have already made it clear that I would have this factory here over my dead body unless they guaranteed to pay the wages in English money!'

Since no-one in the audience was quick enough to reply that deutschmarks might have been a better deal, this got a combined reaction of laughter from those who saw the joke and applause from those who thought that payment in marks might have been a possibility – all far from the usual reception of a Tory MP at North End.

Jack Fudge knew his problems weren't over yet – but he had been to worse meetings that this one. He sat down looking relieved.

Councillor Jones, still angry but glad to have avoided attack upon himself, saved by Jack Fudge's comments, decided that enough was enough. He fielded a few more questions, by now shifting his own position a little closer to the centre of the issue, and closed the debate without even calling Mr Muffle to speak.

The meeting broke up with the public streaming out to their houses or for what remained of pub-hours, the principal guests departing and the Councillor helping the management committee members to sweep the floor of cigarette-ends, match boxes, sweet wrappings and other rubbish dropped during the discussion. It was commonly accepted that cleaning, in circumstances like these, simply couldn't be left for the cleaners the next morning – they would have been outraged and gone straight to their union.

The Mayoral car, in which both Fred Meadows and Mr Muffle had travelled from the Town Hall, was parked next to Jack Fudge's large Volvo Estate. Before any of them got in, the Mayor and Town Clerk accosted the Member of Parliament.

'What's going on?' asked the Mayor, his words decoratively iced with suspicion.

'Well', answered the MP, 'I'm still not entirely convinced – but the more I talk to people, the more I wonder if we shouldn't go for this Zugswang thing. There really is quite a lot of support around the place you know. Perhaps I was a bit hasty before.'

'Ah', replied the Mayor, with certainty, you've been counting the votes in it!'

'Well', mused the other, with a faint smile, 'You do have to take account of these things – and just occasionally it seems right to have a change of heart.'

Fred Meadows peered intently through his end-of-the-nose lenses into the eyes of the Member of Parliament. He could detect no obvious lie in this statement.

They said their good-byes, got into their cars and drove, or were driven, away. The Mayor was almost convinced by the reason given for the change of view. Mr Muffle still very curious – since he saw Jack Fudge as a man with no heart to change and no interest in vote-counting when the Town had always returned a Tory and always would as long as the main opposition parties both insisted upon fielding candidates who cancelled each other out.

The Mayoral car felt hot and stuffy. It was by now getting dark, the evening was one of those when the air was warm and motionless: a match struck to light a cigar in the garden would have burned without needing cupped hands to shield it. At Mr Muffle's suggestion, they got Mr Horrocks to drop them a little short of their destination, at the top of Cobble Lane, so that they could talk things over whilst strolling down to the concrete towpath of the River Septon, and then along it for a while towards the ancient Mercia Bridge. From there they could climb the steps alongside the bridge and then double back to the Town Hall.

The Mayor opened.

'I suppose this does make things a bit easier for you to-morrow. The breakfast news on the radio and the first editions of the Planet will have to say that we finished the meeting a bit in the air – and I was expecting a near lynching.'

The Mayor was joking about the lynching, of course, this being England, but public meetings against something, when the public got too wound-up, did take on that sort of flavour at times.

'Yes', replied Mr Muffle, 'We (he almost felt able to say 'we' at this point and was not rebuffed) did get an easier ride than I expected. But what is Daft Jack up to?'

'Seems obvious enough,' replied the Mayor, though without complete certainty. 'He's realised that his votes at the next election could go up by the number of people who get jobs with Zugswang.'

'It's three years off', answered the Town Clerk, 'and he doesn't have to count votes here anyway. I think there's more to it – but I doubt if we'll ever know.'

'Maybe,' said the Mayor after some thought. 'But the point is that his change of tack makes it easier for me to go along with you tomorrow. Maybe (with a hint of a chuckle) we could send him to explain to Sir Blathwell at Blanks – and to the wretched Town Forum!'

By this time, they had walked far enough around the broad curve of the promenade for the yellow lights strung along the Mercia Bridge to come into full view, reflecting prettily on the surface of the river which hardly rippled. The slow current was broken only by a low island of silt, half covered by willows, on which ducks and swans roosted. The heads of a few pedestrians, strolling into or out of town, could be seen in the light above the bridge parapet and the music of an un-tuned piano, on which a slow tango was almost being played, drifted out into the night. Without any comment, they both thought what a very pleasant place Standing Stillbury was if you had somewhere to live and enough to eat.

Once up the bridge-side steps, used by townspeople for centuries past, they detoured slightly from the route back to the Town Hall for a beer in the Bear Hotel, each feeling a little more relaxed than for some days.

Jack Fudge had not gone home either. He had gone straight from the meeting at North End to the Conservative Club to continue the dangerous, crab-like process of casting-off one shell and growing another. He was well aware that the greatest danger from predators lay during the brief period before the new shell was fully-grown and hardened.

Chapter 12 – Another Kind of Meeting

The next day at 2.00 pm the fifteen members of the Policy Committee of Standing Stillbury Borough Council began to wander into the committee room. There were no apologies for absence. No-one wanted to miss this meeting.

The committee room was next to the mayor's parlour, and oak-panelled and blue-carpeted in similar fashion. But it was much longer and brighter, having the advantage of three tall sash windows which overlooked the well-kept lawns and flower gardens at the back of the Town Hall, a place seldom seen by the rate-payers. The far side of the garden, which ended in a low brick wall, overlooked in turn the River Sefton, far below, with the ancient Mercia Bridge to the right.

Sometimes the Town Hall staff, of both sexes and all ages, played a gentle sort of tennis-ball cricket on the lawn during Summer lunch hours. The typists were allowed a turn at batting, defending wastepaper-basket stumps, and would shriek with mock-terror as the tennis ball, sent down from an underarm delivery, was made to spin sharply from the point on the grass upon which it landed, passing the flailing bat nine times out of ten. You could be out if the wastepaper-basket was hit or if the ball was caught 'one-hand-first-bounce'. It was all played for a laugh and made a very agreeable way to pass an hour on a hot day.

The game wore down the grass in patches and sometimes resulted in the odd rose-head being knocked off. So every now and again they would be banned by the Parks Manager whose men, grumbling about the damage, had to keep the gardens in immaculate condition. But they always crept back after a week or so, guessing rightly that Mr Muffle himself had more sympathy with them than with the complaining gardeners. In return for the Town Clerk's blind-eyed indulgence, they were careful never to embarrass him with the councillors by being late back to their desks on days when there was an afternoon committee meeting in the room overlooking the unofficial pitch.

Once, the Chief Auditor had driven a tennis ball past the fielders and through one of the small window panes of the committee room. A telephone call of some urgency to the Works Department had resulted in it being repaired within twenty-five minutes, just in time for the arrival of some of the elected members who suspected nothing. This was no small indulgence on the part of the works department since, at the time, the average wait for a council house window repair was six weeks. They had chalked up the credit with the audit department, to be cashed in on some future occasion.

The timing of committee meetings at Standing Stillbury was a matter of some small interest. Councils under Conservative control, as this one was, generally preferred evening meetings. In the main, Conservative councillors tended to be self-employed or in jobs which carried responsibilities they durst not abandon too long during the day. Labour councillors preferred daytime meetings. Mostly employees, often trade unionists, they relished their time off work to attend. There were, of course, exceptions within both parties but I have stated the majority position of each at the time of these events.

Throughout Deepshire, most councillors of all parties made full use of the new attendance allowances which had ended their amateur status. A few of the more highly principled, from left and right, firmly refused to claim anything – but they would be gone in a generation and soon everyone would grab everything he or she could get away with. Every few years someone would get too greedy with his or her claims and get sent to prison in disgrace.

For the most part, the allowances would probably have been higher had not an unkind government, which detested local councillors anyhow, insisted that a table of the claims made by the members of every council be published annually in the nearest local newspaper. The Deepshire Planet was always happy to oblige with this. It was one of

the few pieces of council information at which most of the
Town peered intently. For councillors who needed the
money, the trick was to claim as much as possible without
being the councillor who claimed the most. Claiming the
most was an honour they all tried very hard to disclaim.

The attendance allowances had been supposed to tempt
some higher calibre people into council affairs. They
hadn't. They had certainly attracted some people for whom
they formed an appreciable percentage of total income. But
generally speaking they simply shovelled public money to
the same widely varied mix of the capable, the culpable and
the congenital as before. With some noble exceptions,
many people of real worth couldn't abide sitting through
the endless waffle-shop meetings which were necessary to
achieve even the smallest advance in the public affairs of the
Town. This was a harsh view, since, clearly, someone had
to do it, but it was depressingly accurate. You had to have a
mind which could endure the countless deferrals, references
back, points of order and minor acts of party and personal
spite which could make a marathon out of the simplest and
most obvious decisions.

The reason for the Standing Stillbury Policy Committee
meeting at 2.00 pm was, plainly, not to do with the politics
of the controlling party: there was simply too much business
for an evening alone. It would go on to 8.00 pm or 9.00 pm
as it was.

There were weighty agenda items which had been
coming before the Committee for years but which remained
stubbornly unresolved.

A decade before, a team made up of local schoolchildren
had astonished everyone by winning a televised European
fun and games competition – and the large cash prize was
to have been held in trust and spent on a commemorative
fountain which would have immortalised their achievement
and all their names. Even at this time, there was still
argument about the design of the fountain and where in the
Town it should go as the memory of the event faded and the
participants grew up and acquired mortgages and children,
or just left the Town. One had even died.

A local farmer had found and donated to the Council an

extraordinary clutch of amonites and other fossils discovered on his land during the digging of foundations for a
new barn. This was only five years before. The find was of
international importance and photographs of the fossils had
appeared in newspapers all around the world. They were
known as the Stillbury Fossils. It was clear that a modest
investment in the display of the amonites would add to the
Town's attractions both to tourists and scientists. But the
display arrangements were still lost in a treacle of indeci-
sion, argument and reluctance to invest any money. In the
meantime the fossils were on indefinite loan to a grateful
museum in a distant city and some of the less literate
residents had come to believe that the expression 'Stillbury
Fossils' was an official collective name for the councillors.
Some of the more literate thought they were right.

And it seemed to some of the officials that the Town
would never have a car-parking policy of any kind. Year
upon year the Council seemed to veer between allowing
less parking in the Town Centre, in order to support the
shops, and having more parking in the Town Centre, in
order to support the shops. No-one could explain what the
long-term aims of Standing Stillbury's ad hoc decisions on
parking were: of what greater plan they formed a part. In
the meantime, the roads got more clogged and sometimes a
bit less clogged as time passed and this or that new idea was
tried.

The one consistent advance, every year, was in the yard-
age of double yellow lines on the road edges of the Town –
but the more knowing residents had worked out a cunning
strategy to deal with them. You simply parked on the lines
at will and then switched on the flashing hazard warning
lights with which modern cars are equipped. At times whole
rows of cars with flashing hazard lights could be seen at the
edges of narrow streets, with not a traffic warden in sight. It
was a splendid wheeze. As long as the hazard warning lights
were flashing, you could get away with at least an hour's
illegal and obstructive parking in the centre of Standing
Stillbury. With the car-boot left open as well, to give a spur-
ious impression of 'loading and/or unloading', two hours or
more.

But the biggest and first business of this day was the Zugswang factory.

At the head of the table, which formed the cross-piece of a T, sat Jervis Boddington, Chairman of the Committee. This role went with his position as leader of the Council. The Mayor was nominally just an ordinary member of this forum – though his personal seniority within his party and his network of old alliances made him more equal than most.

To the right of Jervis Boddington sat Mr Muffle, Town Clerk and thus chief advisor to the councillors. To HIS right sat a harassed-looking committee clerk, piles of loose papers and files in front of him to be extracted quickly in the event, and there were usually many, of some point of fact being disputed. A small notebook lay ready to record the main points of discussion and the decisions.

To the left of the Chairman was the Borough Treasurer, Mr Tite, and further left his Chief Accountant in support, with more piles of papers. Behind this top-table group, the wall was covered with an assortment of plans and charts thought necessary to illustrate the business to follow.

The councillors, each with bulky sets of committee papers sent out the week before, mostly un-read until the item in question came up on the agenda, sat on both sides of the upright part of the T. The remaining chief officers and departmental heads, the Council's paid officials, sat on chairs behind the Councillors, ready to advise on or account for business done or neglected since the last meeting. It was no exaggeration to say that this gathering was costing the ratepayers of Standing Stillbury over £500 per hour in salaries and councillors' attendance allowances.

The senior officials, a very mixed bunch indeed sitting behind the Councillors, were sometimes referred to by the junior staff as the crazy gang – and not without a certain wry affection. Almost all of them – architect, planner, housing manager, road engineer, medical officer and a good few others – had once been extremely good at what they did professionally.

The problem was that, in order to get to the top of their professions, in the small pond of Standing Stillbury at least, they had all had to change from doing their jobs to managing numbers of other people who did similar jobs. This was a vast step for which some were well-fitted and others not. Some crossed the management divide rather well, of course, but others simply couldn't cope. They sometimes carried on for years, deceiving themselves that they were running a council department when the department was running them. Some were too easily bullied by stronger-minded subordinates; some locked themselves away in large offices, shielded by fierce secretaries, and communicated with their staff by flurries of memoranda – most of which were ignored as the staff tried to get on with their jobs, rudderless, as best they could.

There was an element of Greek Tragedy about some of these appointments. The most ill-judged were obviously wrong even when they were made, but the tradition of preference for seniority and technical or professional expertise was so deeply ingrained that an obvious lack of skill in handling people would be over-looked by earnest panels of elected members as they interviewed the applicants. For a talented, gregarious manager at position number 3 in a department to apply for the vacant top job in competition with a technically able but personally inept manager at position 2 was regarded as near treachery. The brash hopeful was usually ignored and would have to take a job elsewhere to further his career.

Even when things went badly wrong, the councillors were reluctant to act decisively, with one curious exception: they were always willing to get rid of an entertainments officer who overspent his budget by a few thousand. They could grasp that sort of nettle and understand what had gone wrong – and entertainments officers tended to be bright, extrovert sorts of people who came and went, getting on with things quickly and treading on a few toes in the process. They had an almost self-assumed air of expendability about themselves.

But a solemn highways engineer whose staff had allowed £250,000 of overspending on a road project was quite beyond the reach of the councillors. Few of them could argue over the technicalities he would put up in justification, or match the donnish erudition with which the explanation would be offered. Indeed, the worst offenders in this respect usually ended their careers with an appearance in the honours list, an MBE or OBE appended to names quite unsullied by the financial chaos they had caused.

And there were some able managers amongst the senior officers, it must be said. This latter group was not only interested in the idea of attracting investment to the Town, something quite new to most of them, but was even thinking how they might help the Town Clerk to achieve it. The less imaginative would listen out of curiosity but assume that the whole affair had nothing to do with them personally.

As soon as the tea was brought in, an essential without which the meeting could not start, the Chairman sought and received without dissent, permission to sign as correct the minutes of the previous month's meeting.

He then moved to the main item. The Zugswang Components Company of Dusseldorf.

Each member had a copy of Mr Muffle's four-page report on the subject, outlining the facts and recommending that the Council contact the Company to discuss the site at North End. So controversial was this particular report that a few of them had even read it before coming to the meeting – a most unusual circumstance.

Jervis Boddington had no clear ideas about Zugswang. But merely opening the discussion gave him a pleasant feeling of dabbling in international affairs, the more so for their taking place in a town which still had a few inhabitants who had never been to either the seaside or London.

'We've all heard about this in the last week or so', he began. 'and I gather that the public meeting last night wasn't quite so hostile as we'd expected.'

'And,' he went on, leaning back, hands on jacket lapels above a large stomach-line, as if imparting some news of the utmost confidentiality, 'I gather the Member of Parliament has shifted his ground a bit.' He had actually read this in the first edition of the Deepshire Planet which came out at around 1.30 pm each day.

At this point he turned to Mr Muffle to fill in the details.

Mr Muffle was well aware that the change in Jack Fudge's position might be of importance as some members of the Committee were personal friends or political cronies of the MP. But he was also aware of the need not to present this change in a way which was damaging. Having turned once, he feared, the Member of Parliament might turn again. In fact that wouldn't now happen – but Mr Muffle had no way of knowing it.

'Yes, the meeting turned out a bit easier than expected. Jack Fudge didn't totally shift his position, he rather reserved it. But he was generous enough to suggest that a hasty decision either way might be unwise given that there could be some hundreds of jobs in it.'

One or two heads nodded wisely at this statement as some of the members grasped the care with which the Town Clerk had chosen his words.

'What', came a voice from down the table, 'can we do about it now? Aren't the Concrete Hardening lot after this one as well?'

There were broad grins followed by one or two mock hisses at the mention of Concrete Hardening. By a sort of local convention, this was almost obligatory in Standing Stillbury circles: council, business and even social. Concrete Hardening was perceived as an upstart rival to the County Town's pre-eminence. It was depicted as being full of 'rabbit-hutch' housing estates, soulless factories and endless new roads – not the sort of thing which was regarded as right for Deepshire at all. The loudest hisses usually came from those who had never actually been the ten miles along the road to see for themselves. Those who did usually returned looking quite thoughtful. Some of them even got jobs there and did very well for themselves.

And Concrete Hardening had recently stunned its detractors by winning the Blooming Britain Competition, ahead of Standing Stillbury which had prided itself on its floral attractions for decades. This occurrence had caused astonishment on a national scale. In a small and rare spark of generosity from the one town to the other, the organiser of Standing Stillbury's Blooming Britain Committee had immediately telephoned and offered congratulations to his rivals. But gestures of that kind were still quite unusual at the time of this story.

The question about Concrete Hardening had, as procedure dictated, been aimed at the Chairman but, as practicality dictated, he deflected it to Mr Muffle with a slight inclination of his head. A good Town Clerk always knows when a question has been so deflected and never annoys his chairman by jumping in beforehand or, worse, embarrassing him by a delayed reaction.

'I am quite sure that Concrete Hardening will be interested', responded the Town Clerk, 'and I must admit to being a bit worried about that. This has been running for quite a while now and, since you haven't yet agreed anything, the Company doesn't actually know of our interest.'

(In fact, Herr Grossemann was at that moment reading a telexed copy of the article about the meeting at North End, on the front page of that day's Deepshire Planet. One of his staff in the Concrete Hardening Hotel, researching the type of labour available, had bought the newspaper and thought his boss might be interested. He made a note to thank his subordinate for his initiative in sending it.)

There followed some free-wheeling debate which quickly got out of control under Jervis Boddington's limited chairmanship skills. Several simultaneous conversations developed and the Committee Clerk, raising his eyes to heaven as he lowered his pencil to the table, waited for order to return.

But the comments were less hostile than at the informal meeting the week before. One or two of the more impenetrable were still making inane remarks about the long-answered questions of effluent in the sewers and drains and pressure on the roads – but there was more recognition of the new jobs involved and of the softening of Jack Fudge's attitude. It wasn't easy, since the directors of Blank's Bearings still had some friends in the room, but a sort of view that was typical of Standing Stillbury politics began to emerge, slowly.

That view was not a wholehearted endorsement of Mr Muffle's plans to lure Zugswang to the Town. It was more an acknowledgement that they might all be criticised if they didn't make some sort of effort. So they grudgingly began to concede that they probably should.

'But what', persisted the councillor who had first asked the question, some order now having returned to the meeting, 'should we be doing about it?'

A languid silence fell around the table. It was still warm and sunny in the late afternoon and a blue-bottle droned loudly, trapped between the overlapping panes of a half-opened sash window.

After some seconds of rare silence Mr Muffle made an extra recommendation, one not printed in his report. 'You know, I don't think we can get them here in a hurry after all the time they've had to think about Concrete Hardening. I think we are going to have to get on a plane to Dusseldorf and see them at their place – quickly.'

This time, there wasn't just a languid silence around the table, but a shocked, electrified sort of silence. The two types of silence are quite different. Several pairs of eyes opened wide. Jervis Boddington's jaw fell open for just a moment. The Borough Treasurer's mouth changed shape to a sort of 'o' as he sucked in breath quickly and audibly.

This required real decision-making.

Further down the agenda was a collection of items involving considerable expenditure for the coming year on the attendance of chief officers and committee chairmen at the annual conferences of a number of professional associations. There was the Health Officers' Association, the Chartered Housing Managers, the Weights and Measures Consortium, the Street Lighting Association and the National Society for Digging Up New Road Surfaces for Cable Repairs – and several more of that kind.

These events would take away various chief officers and their wives, with the appropriate committee chairmen and their wives, to large, expensive hotels in pleasant seaside towns around Britain for a week or so, during which there would be brief readings of papers on this or that technical aspect of the profession's work and a good deal of golfing, sightseeing, partying and general socialising, some of it presided over by the Mayor of the host-town who would delight at all the extra business – in hotels, restaurants,

shops and leisure facilities – being brought in for the benefit
of his rate-payers.

The beneficiaries of this largesse, paid for by the rate-
payers of Standing Stillbury, became quite impassioned if
the expenditure was ever questioned, each pleading that the
exchange of professional views at his particular conference
was essential to his work for the Council. Those chief
officers who got two conferences in a single year were
greatly envied by those of their colleagues who got just one.
Sometimes, when they came back, they produced a report
on the proceedings for their committees, sometimes not.

But the idea of sending people abroad, in an aeroplane,
was unique in the annals of the Council. It was the sort of
thing Concrete Hardening Council did – and even Deepshire County Council occasionally. (Admittedly, usually in
a biplane in the latter case) But not Standing Stillbury.
Hence the shocked silence at what Mr Muffle had said.

Jervis Boddington was the first to speak. Although, like
many small business-cum-professional men of his kind, he
had joined the Council to cut a swathe through the profligacy of the Town Hall, he was not slow to seize an
opportunity. He took the initiative.

'Look', he opened with transparent casualness, 'suppose
we do send a delegation – I suppose it would have to be the
Town Clerk and me – do you think they would see us at this
stage? And how long would we need to be away?'

At this there were some dark looks from down the
table. Several committee members were coming to the conclusion, without yet so declaring, that their own importance
in local affairs was such that they could hardly be omitted
from any delegation to Dusseldorf. They were not going to
leave the Town Clerk and Jervis Boddington with such rich
pickings for themselves. Why, they might even be photo-
graphed by the Planet, setting off for the airport from Standing Stillbury Railway Station, looking mysterious and
international.

As these thoughts flickered through their minds, one or
two members shifted uneasily as they remembered how, the
previous year, they, like most of Deepshire's Members of
Parliament, had failed to react with much energy or fire to

British Rail's proposal to end their through train service to London. Their indifference had been met with astonishment and glee by British Rail officials who had expected a political battering from a county town which had enjoyed the prestige of a London link for decades. So the through-service had been lost. Now the members, or some of them, realised they would have to make at least one change of trains before they got near any airport.

But that twinge of conscience quickly died down. An international visit! From Standing Stillbury! The idea began to gain appeal rapidly. Maybe even the wives could come! First one, then another made his claim.

The Borough Treasurer was still pursing his lips. But now his eyes became as round as his mouth as the new-found inclination for foreign travel erupted amongst the members.

This was not what Mr Muffle had in mind at all. He had assumed that he and the Mayor would go, accepting Jervis Boddington with as good a will as possible if he insisted; perhaps even Jack Fudge if he came around fully to their view. But they all wanted to go to Dusseldorf.

But something had to be decided quickly. Mr Muffle looked despairingly at the length of the agenda which remained to be dealt with. He whispered to Jervis Boddington who called the meeting to order once again. 'Do I take it', asked the Chairman, 'that you all favour trying to get the Zugswang factory in Standing Stillbury?'

Each committee member raised a hand. This time even the waverers had lost all their doubts.

'And', went on the Chairman, 'Do I take it you all want to go to Dusseldorf?'

Each committee member raised a hand.

'And finally', observed the Chairman, 'some of you seem, if I hear rightly, to be suggesting that we take wives along.'

'Yes!' chorused most of the voices in the room.

'Right', concluded Jervis Boddington, 'let's have a show of hands from those who can come, with wives.' Not a single wife had been asked about her participation in the visit but, in a frenzy of anxiousness not to miss out, they were all volunteered.

'Very well, it's fifteen members, fifteen wives, Mr Muffle and Mrs Muffle, so we need arrangements made for thirty two.'

Mr Tite who, up to this point had been frantically guessing at the cost of the members' madness, suddenly wondered how he was going to explain to Mrs Tite that he and she would not be going. But it was too late.

Mr Muffle left the room for a few minutes as the agenda was resumed in the rather flat atmosphere which now descended upon the room. Nothing else for discussion seemed so much fun as this. He leapt up the wide stairway to his first floor office and called in Miss Peeves.

'Listen', he began, sounding slightly agitated (he was quite shocked at the success of his own proposals) 'we need to get plane tickets to Dusseldorf for thirty-two people as soon as possible – and at the same time I want you to telephone Zugswang Components and ask them as a matter of urgency if they can receive a party of 32 from the Council – talk to the Managing Director's Secretary or whoever can speak English – there must be somebody there. Can you do that?'

Miss Peeves stood motionless, her mouth and eyes wide open in pale imitation of Mr Tite a few minutes before.

She finally spoke. 'You mean plane tickets to Germany, and telephoning abroad?'

Miss Peeves had never bought plane tickets or telephoned abroad before. It seemed terrifying.

'Yes, yes,' replied the Town Clerk impatiently. 'Just go to a travel agent for the tickets – that place in the High Street, what's their name? They'll be able to fix it and send us the bill afterwards. And just ask international directory enquiries for Zugswang of Dusseldorf and look in the front of the 'phone book for the Germany code. It'll be 010 something or other.'

'And then you have to match up when we arrive at Dusseldorf with the visit to the company. Perhaps they'll send a coach to the airport to meet us. Give it a try – but I'll have to go now, we've hardly started the agenda. Come in to the meeting later and tell me how you've got on – Oh, and we'll need a hotel as well and some German money –

about a thousand pounds worth should be ample.'

Before Miss Peeves could say more, the Town Clerk was out of the office and bounding down the stairs again. Miss Peeves was left clenching and unclenching her fists, her left foot drumming impotently on the carpet. She hadn't got to be the Town Clerk's Secretary in order to talk to Germans and organise foreign travel. But she supposed she had better get on with it and walked towards the the Town Clerk's telephone. If she really had to do this, it would, like all out-of-the-ordinary things, be kept confidential from the rest of the staff for as long as possible. Being in the know was, after all, one of the few perks of an increasingly irritating job.

Chapter 13 – Calling Germany

The telephone made a strange bleeping noise. She thought it must be engaged. But then, after a few moments, it clicked and a bright female voice said 'Guten tag – Zugswang'.

Somewhat timidly Miss Peeves, who spoke no language other than her own, asked, slowly and deliberately, '*DO YOU SPEAK ENGLISH?*'

'Yes, certainly', replied the voice with very little German accent and sounding almost puzzled at such a silly question, 'How can I help you?'

Miss Peeves breathed out with some relief. Perhaps this wouldn't be so bad.

'It's Standing Stillbury Council here – in England, you know – I'm 'phoning from the Town Hall. My name is Miss Peeves.'

'Ye-es?' said the other, slowly, making the word a question.

'Well', continued Miss Peeves, 'the Town Clerk has asked me to see if we could organise a visit to your company.'

'Ah!' replied the voice, brightly again, 'I am sure that will be a pleasure. Please wait on the telephone and I will put you through to someone who is arranging this.'

The telephone made a another clicking noise and, after a minute or two, another voice came on to the line – another female voice.

'Good morning, the switchboard tells me you are liking to arrange a visit to the Company. You are from a rathaus in England I think?'

Miss Peeves blinked. She didn't like the sound of rathaus at all.

'No, no! I am from the Town Hall at Standing Stillbury, the famous historic town in Deepshire. The Town Clerk said I was to ask if we could visit you.'

'Town Clerk?' said the other voice, carefully repeating

the pronunciation, then, with an apparent flash of inspiration, 'This is like a burgermeister, yes?'

This time Miss Peeves had the flash of inspiration, managing to separate out 'burg' and 'meister' and concluding that the two together sounded like someone who was in a town and master of it.

'Yes, yes,' she volunteered, quite pleased with herself, 'I'm sure that's about the same thing.'

'Good', replied the voice, 'we are always very pleased to arrange this – we have had visits from other English towns and you will be welcome as well. How many people will be in your group and which day will you come?'

'Fifteen councillors, the Town Clerk and all their wives', answered Miss Peeves, 'and', rummaging through the Council diary, 'next Wednesday would be best for us if you can manage it.' She was slightly bemused at the success of the call. She had expected to have to make some sort of case to justify the visit – but none had been demanded. Standing Stillbury Council was obviously to be accommodated in its wish and allowed into the Zugswang Works.

'That will be fine', replied the lady from Germany, 'but could you please be sure to send a list with the names and titles of all your people.'

'Yes, certainly, and thank you very much. Could you possibly tell me of a hotel where I could arrange for the councillors to stay the night before?'

'Of course', replied the other, 'If you leave this with me I will call you back when I have found out which one has enough rooms free and I will book them for the night before if that would be helpful to you.'

'That would be marvellous,' replied Miss Peeves, by now gushing with gratitude and relief combined.

The call was ended.

After that, the arrangement of the air tickets seemed simplicity itself, Miss Peeves even having the presence of mind to swear the local travel agent to secrecy – a demand to which he readily acceded in return for such good business. To arrange this detail was no part of the brief given to her by the Town Clerk, but Miss Peeves had an instinctive and acute sense of secrecy where the arrangements surrounding Mr Muffle's and her work were concerned. She sensed it should be secret and wasn't wrong.

The most puzzling part of the arrangement was not, in fact, fixing things up with the Germans. It was ordering Mr Muffle's German money from the local bank. Miss Peeves had never done this before, either. It took a little while before she grasped what the cashier on the currency desk was trying to explain.

'You mean', said Miss Peeves, finally, 'that you charge a fixed fee AND a pro-rata commission for doing it, and then give us so many Deutchmarks to the pound – but if we bring any back, then you give us back 10% less English money back per mark than when we started?'

'Yes', replied the cashier, mildly wondering how this could be thought a matter to be queried.

Miss Peeves was reasonably numerate. 'But at that rate, if we started with £1,000 or so, we would only have to make seven or eight changes of currency through your bank and it would all be gone – even if we didn't spend any.'

'Yes, of course', replied the cashier, getting slightly impatient, still quite failing to understand how such an arrangement might be questioned. The time had not yet arrived when banks had to compete for this sort of business. Highly advantageous transactions of this kind were still assumed to be a God-given right, not to be haggled over by the mere users of the service who were expected to be both silently acquiescent and even grateful.

'Oh!' replied Miss Peeves, slightly deflated, at a loss for what more she could say, her education having been expanded considerably in the space of five minutes.

Then the lady at Zugswang called back.

'We have arranged your rooms – the Hotel Unzicker in the centre of Dusseldorf – they will allow you the same corporate rates that we pay. And we will have a coach to meet you at the airport and take you there, and then bring you to us at nine the next morning.

Miss Peeves was delighted. Things just didn't go that smoothly as a rule. Corporate rates was a new expression which sounded as if it might mean cheaper – and a coach to take them to the works. What could possibly go wrong?!

Brimming with self importance and secret knowledge, she strode down the wide Town Hall stairway to the committee room.

As she entered, the conversation stopped and everyone in the room looked up at her in expectancy. Some of the officers, those who had been on the rough edge of her tongue when wielded, frequently, in the name of the Town Clerk, secretly hoped she had made a mess of her task. The councillors were agog with anticipation of a foreign visit and hoped she had succeeded.

'Well', she said, 'That's all fixed. They'll see you on Wednesday at nine in the morning. I've fixed up rooms at the Hotel Unzicker in the middle of Dusseldorf the night before – and I got corporate rates out of them. You'll have to fly from Luton at 4.00 pm on the Tuesday and the Company will provide a coach to meet you at Dusseldorf Airport.'

There were gasps of astonishment and admiration. How efficient. And corporate rates out of the hotel.

'That', some thought secretly, 'is why we've put up with her all this time. She must be able to speak a bit of German'.

One asked if she did. In a brief flash of time she came up with the answer. 'Only very little.' There were knowing looks around the table. Clearly, the Town Clerk's Secretary was hiding her light under a bushel, understating her abilities with typical English modesty. But her answer had actually been quite true. She did only speak very little German. She had learned it that day. It was consisted of the words rathaus and burgermeister – and she still didn't know what the former meant and, without any serious consequence, hadn't realised that the latter meant mayor and not town clerk.

The remaining business of the meeting was ruthlessly deferred to a later date. Long awaited grant applications for the restoration of domestic property and listed historic buildings, endless staff claims for salary increases, adjustments to the budgets of spending departments and a great deal else were dumped in the excitement of a trip to Germany.

Mr Muffle left quickly to have the Borough Surveyor draw up plans of a factory site at the North End Industrial Estate.

Chapter 14 – It's a Deal!

Tuesday of the following week was an important day in the history of the County of Deepshire.

That afternoon, a British Airways Boeing 737 flew into Luton Airport from Dusseldorf and discharged a full load of passengers. Amongst them were Herr Grossemann and Herr Pfennig. They cleared customs, strolled through the concourse and then outside, to be met by the driver of the Concrete Hardening official car. They exchanged cheerful greetings – having got to know the driver quite well by now – and were ushered in, their luggage being taken from them and quickly packed in the boot.

A coach carrying fifteen councillors from Standing Stillbury, their wives and Mr and Mrs Muffle, passed by as this was happening, on its way to arrivals. The men were wearing best suits of varying quality and fit. The most impressive suits came from the Town's last remaining privately-owned men's outfitter – Kernel's – which stubbornly clung to existence as the others of its kind faded away before competition from the chain stores from which the other, cheaper, suits had been bought. But expensive or cheap, suits don't fly well and they would all look pretty crumpled a few hours later.

The wives were mostly sporting hats of assorted luridity, of the type which would be worn at the annual mayor-making ceremony. They had got together and decided that hats would be right for a visit of such moment.

Some of the coach passengers glanced down at the parked car and at the Germans getting in. Herr Pfennig glanced up at the coach. He noticed that it belonged to a company from Standing Stillbury and recalled with some pleasure the impressions of his recent visit to that Town – but he assumed that the passengers were holiday-makers on

their way to one of the more vulgar Spanish resorts or
something of that sort.

Neither party had the faintest idea of the identity or
purpose of the other. The visit of the Germans was to remain secret for the next few hours. The Standing Stillbury
visit, the councillors had accepted with reluctance, on Mr
Muffle's advice (which bore out Miss Peeves' earlier judgment) had also been treated as secret. This was ostensibly
for reasons of commercial confidentiality – a portentious
phrase which the councillors had swallowed without realising what it meant. In fact, Mr Muffle was becoming more
and more uneasy about public reaction to the number of
people enjoying the jaunt. He had firmly suppressed any
lingering idea of asking the Deepshire Planet to take a
picture of the party leaving on their mission. Unfortunately,
however, secrecy was a little less easy to maintain in the
older of the two towns.

The coach went on to disgorge its passengers. There was
some time to wait. They would be flying on the same
aircraft as that which had brought the Zugswang Directors
in. It would be cleaned, re-provisioned and re-fuelled in the
space of an hour or so.

The Councillors began to enjoy themselves. Food and
drinks of all kinds, some strong, some not, were ordered in
the departure lounge cafes. Newspapers and books were
bought for the flight. Mr Muffle observed with mild distaste
the propensity of confirmed half-pint-of-bitter drinkers to
order large scotches when they were imbibing on the rates.

The Concrete Hardening car got back to that town just
about as BA Flight 6460 was taking off from Luton. As
usual, the two Germans were put up at the Concrete
Hardening Hotel, but before going to their rooms, they
were met by Henry Morgan and Brian Fichtl with whom
more pleasantries and greetings were exchanged.

'We know you'll want a couple of hours, but just come
and have a look at the room layout before you go upstairs,'
suggested the Chief Executive.

'We've got everything lined up for tomorrow but we
thought a little party tonight was justified!'

The Germans followed their hosts across the foyer and

entered a private room festooned with British and German flags, the centre-piece of which was a magnificently laid-out table ready for a celebration for twenty. Herr Pfennig glanced quizzically at Herr Grossemann. Herr Grossemann beamed with delight. So Herr Pfennig did likewise. 'That', said the Chairman of Zugswang Components, 'looks splendid'. 'We shall see you this evening.' They headed for the lift. It was of English manufacture but nevertheless worked perfectly, first time.

Everything went smoothly at Dusseldorf. The party – and it had become such in two senses of the word – emerged from the aircraft and was not troubled by the German customs officers. It seemed that the Zugswang Company had made it known that they were expected and the Company's guests were obviously treated with respect at their local airport. Councillors and wives and the Muffles were met in the departure lounge by a blonde young lady who spoke perfect English, welcomed them politely and directed them to a hired executive coach which would get them to the Hotel Unzicker in 20 minutes.

From the speeding vehicle, the visitors soaked in a passing scene which consisted of first neat and tidy houses, then neat and tidy shops and then office blocks of all sizes and shapes, set in a landscape which at first puzzled them. Then it dawned. There wasn't a single piece of litter in sight. Anywhere. Clearly, they were far from home.

At the hotel, things were just as efficiently organised. The Manager, noticing such a large party of English guests on the day's reservations, had made a point of being present to welcome them personally. Like the airport officials, he too regarded guests of Zugswang Components as people of substance. As they arrived he stood in the centre of the magnificent hotel reception area – a place which had a strange resemblance to the reception area at Blank's Bearings back in Standing Stillbury – except that in this reception area, there were a lot more people doing business.

The Council party was, by this time, almost beside itself with self-importance. The councillors puffed out their chests. Their wives preened. Some of them began to understand why the Euro MP for Deepshire, Sir Wykeham

Fagge, was prepared to undertake such strenuous exertions for the few weeks before each five-yearly election in order to keep his seat. This was living. 'What', thought one or two, looking around in astonishment, 'have we been doing for the last twenty years?' Whole new vistas for the conduct of council business on a European scale began opening up.

'Good evening, ladies and gentlemen', began the Manager. 'It is a great pleasure to welcome you all to the Hotel Unzicker. As soon as you have registered, my staff are on hand to show you to your rooms. Please use the telephones by your beds to call my personal office if you have any problem at all.'

The Mayor having been edged to the front of the party by the others, wasn't quite sure of the level of reply appropriate for this greeting – which seemed rather inflated: the hotel had 5 stars and over 300 bedrooms after all – but decided upon a 'Thank you very much, we are sure that everything in your hotel will be perfect.' The Manager beamed. The chances were it would be.

By this time things were beginning to happen in Concrete Hardening. The Chief Executive and his leading councillors, together with Warren Clews-Lessley and local MP Janus Berkley were standing behind their chairs in a private dining room at the Concrete Hardening Hotel. After a minute or two Herr Grossemann and Herr Pfennig walked in and were shown to their places to a hearty round of applause. Everyone was smiling.

The party sat and a splendid dinner began, one of those occasions when the room is filled with happy and uninhibited talk and the hours flash past like coaches in the outside lane. Smoked salmon was followed by fillet of beef, cooked rare and almost willing to part before the knife touched the surface. And that was followed by a pie made with locally-picked whimberries – the picking of which, in the wild, on the slopes of the South Deepshire Hills, had been arranged by the Head Chef earlier that day, an hour or so before he personally made the pie. The climax was the Deepshire Blue Cheese which, it had been noted, the Germans had enjoyed during their visit to the races. It came round and heavy, its orangey-yellow marked by the veins of blue bacteria which gave it its distinct flavour. The food was all very English and the Germans felt they had been privileged to enjoy something quite out of the ordinary. They had. The tourists didn't get much of this. And the best German wines the hotel had been able to buy-in flowed freely. The patriotism of the Labour Group on Concrete Hardening District Council extended to food – but not quite as far as wine.

Everyone relaxed completely. There were toasts across the table – some less coherent than others. But no-one minded. By the end of the evening everyone was contented and mellow and you wouldn't have thought that our side and their's had been to war twice in the eye-blink of eternity we call a century.

In Dusseldorf, a similar sort of scene was unfolding. The Standing Stillbury councillors had arranged for their own private dining room on the grounds that the crucial nature of their visit justified a minor extravagance of this nature. It never occurred to them to ask anyone from the Zugswang Company to join them. They just had a good, and increasingly riotous evening as unlimited supplies of wine flowed in their direction, punctuated by excellent food which no-one would quite remember the next morning. They did, however, vaguely recall that Germany seemed to have available wines of rather better quality than the anonymous Liebfraumilch which, very wisely, they dump on us in huge quantities whilst keeping the best of their own production for home consumption. One or two of the waiters, without visibly betraying their thoughts, even to each other, wondered if the party wasn't a little less 'anstandig' than the general run of visiting parties to the Zugswang Works – but the idea was as quickly shrugged off as they concentrated, very professionally, on their business.

By the time they all went to bed, inhibitions were so far lowered that a curious and unfortunate thing happened. Two of the Councillors, whose names will not be mentioned, whose matrimonial infidelities with each other's wives had been successfully kept private back at home (a most rare achievement), lost just enough of their judgment to make the fatal mistake of carrying these affairs into their hotel bedrooms. They assumed they would be able to switch rooms unobserved in the morning. It never works. Since all four had to be woken from a still mildly drunken stupor, they faced first disbelief and then an even split between bawdy hilarity (from the men) and virtuous outrage (from the women).

In fact, the men were the ones who were outraged – but, being men, they felt they had to condone the offence over crude guffaws and knowing grins to each other. The women, or some of them at least, desperately envied the errant wives but felt that, as women, they just HAD to be outraged. Nevertheless, word of this misadventure got back to Standing Stillbury by telephone before everyone had even got down to reception.

Of course, the two men brazened it out pretty well. The two wives stuck together, in unusual silence, over breakfast and for the remainder of the visit.

Zugswang had been as good as its word. The smart coach and the well-spoken guide arrived at the hotel entrance as promised. They dragged themselves into the vehicle over the space of fifteen minutes. It is a wonder of modern life just how long it takes to get a group of people into a coach – even when they are all present together and waiting for the vehicle. In this case the celebrations of the previous night had impaired the fitness for travel and the enthusiasm of the intended passengers to a greater or lesser degree.

Mr Muffle, though, and Fred Meadows to some general surprise, had stayed very sober. Neither of them had forgotten the purpose of the visit and both were now anxious to get on with the business of the day.

In Concrete Hardening, the business of the day had already started. In a large public room of the Concrete Hardening Hotel, tables and chairs had been set at one end as if for their occupants to address a public meeting of some kind. Small wooden blocks at each of the table places were sprouting miniature German and Union flags. People were starting to trickle into the room to occupy seats, arranged in theatre style, in neat rows, facing the tables. Two television crews were quickly arranging their equipment as if to record some sort of event. Some of the people entering the room had that indefinable, slightly-less-than-respectable air about them which suggests a journalist.

The Standing Stillbury coach quickly reached the entrance to the Zugswang Works. Like Blank's Bearings, the Company had a gatehouse – but there the resemblance ended. The uniformed guard in this gatehouse was not reading a newspaper. He had before him a clearly typed note which explained who would be in the coach. He was awaiting their arrival and as soon as the vehicle came into view he stepped out of his shelter and, after briefly confirming things with the driver, smartly raised the barrier arm and, to the astonishment of the passengers, those not asleep at least, saluted as they went past.

The coach was directed to the entrance to a spotlessly clean, newish-looking factory block. A man in his mid-thirties, perhaps a little younger than Mr Muffle had expected, was waiting to greet them. He announced himself as Herr Becker and after addressing them all in, once again, excellent English, invited them into a large room where coffee was served.

Mr Muffle and the Mayor had not been very sure of the precise arrangements for a day like this but, being in a foreign country, were resolved to follow the lead given by their hosts. It seemed a little odd for coffee to be followed by a fifteen minute talk by Herr Becker on the history of Zugswang Components, accompanied by frequent references to productivity and sales charts fixed to the walls – and detailed descriptions of some highly technical products made by the Company for the motor industry worldwide. But then the visitors were presented with beautifully printed brochures, all in English, about every public aspect of Zugswang.

At around this point, Mr Muffle, and Fred Meadows, began to think that they should perhaps be talking about the Company's hoped-for interest in the field at the North End of Standing Stillbury. But before the Town Clerk could even pull the site plans from the briefcase which he, alone amongst the party carried, they found themselves being led briskly to the production area of the factory building.

In itself, this was interesting enough. In fact it was very

interesting. A fairly cheerful, youngish, crowd of workers was engaged in carefully producing a variety of motor parts – in this building mostly for car heating systems. Everyone was dressed cleanly and neither a metal or plastic shaving nor a discarded screw, nut or bolt of any kind could be seen on the spotless floor. People who were evidently senior managers appeared here and there and appeared actually to speak to the people making the products. The senior managers were dressed in the same white jackets as everyone else. And everyone seemed to be happily intent upon doing his or her job.

Herr Becker, who himself seemed to know most of the people at work, explained all of these arrangements with obvious pride as he led his charges through a tour which ran through first one hour and then, a shade tiringly, another. This really was a very large factory.

The Town Clerk and Fred Meadows were by this time getting anxious and one or two of the more perceptive councillors were casting the occasional inquiring glance at them. Was it not time to talk business?

Several of the wives were beginning to look thoroughly discomforted. They had not previously experienced a standard factory tour (something every large company in the world believes to be unique to itself) which can be a wearisome experience as the enthusiasm of the hosts is weighed in the balance against the indifference of the visitors. They mostly kept quiet though, thinking that the men, as always, knew best.

The television cameras began to roll in the Concrete Hardening Hotel as people took their places on the stage and the seats facing them filled so that late-comers were left standing at the back. Reporters took out their notebooks. The room was filled with the beehive-like noise of subdued but excited conversation.

By this time, Mr Muffle and Fred Meadows had decided that some initiative must be taken. Perhaps this was how the Germans did business but enough was enough. The gruelling factory tour, with its non-stop commentary, had ended and the guests from Standing Stillbury were relieved to have been offered drinks and then lunch in a pleasantly furnished room which overlooked a lake which had been created at the front of the Zugswang Works. But Herr Becker seemed to be doing no more than enjoying their company. He was casually moving around, chatting in turn with this or that guest, even flattering them gently but making no attempt to raise the business of the day.

So they cornered him. It was done politely enough. But they steered him to a corner and make it clear that they wanted to talk business.

Herr Becker was happy to talk business. 'What business exactly? How can I help?'

'The new factory in England', cut in Fred Meadows quickly. 'And where it is going to go.'

'Ah', replied Herr Becker, light and understanding appearing on his face. 'Of course!'

The other two looked relieved.

'As a matter of fact', went on Herr Becker, 'I think we could show you something of considerable interest. Could you both come with me for a moment while the others continue with lunch?'

'Yes, of course', the Mayor and Town Clerk replied as one, each feeling that the visit might be about to take on some purpose.

They made their excuses, which were accepted by all except Jervis Boddington who insisted upon joining them. There would be no credit gained in Germany without the Leader of the Council sharing in it.

Herr Becker led them along a corridor into a spacious room in which several senior executives of the Company and some of the production staff were congregated around a large television screen of some kind. Some of them nodded amiably towards the newcomers and one or two greeted them with, 'Guten tag'. Herr Becker cheerfully introduced them as visitors from Standing Stillbury, in England, at which a few more friendly greetings, in English, were lobbed in their direction – although both the Mayor and Mr Muffle uneasily wondered why all these people hadn't ALREADY known who they were.

'Look', said Herr Becker, pointing to the screen, 'This has been highly secret up to now but, since you are here, we are happy to share some good news with you.'

The three visitors peered at the television. Something was happening in a large room at the end of which was a stage with people making some sort of announcement. There seemed to be television cameras in the room and people in the audience taking notes. Fred Meadows peered even more closely and nudged Mr Muffle. 'Good God! Isn't that Henry Morgan from Concrete Hardening?'

Mr Muffle peered more closely. 'Yes – but what's he doing on TV here?'

The answer was unfolding as the question was asked.

The crowd of reporters and cameramen at the Concrete Hardening Hotel listened intently as Henry Morgan unveiled the latest news of industry coming to the Town. Zugswang Components of Dusseldorf, after weeks of private negotiations, had finally agreed that their UK factory was to be in Concrete Hardening. There would be at least 500 new jobs and as many supplies as possible would be bought from nearby companies, some of which would also have to increase employment in consequence.

The Standing Stillbury jaws dropped as they pressed closer to the screen, unaware in their shock and discomfiture that they had edged some of their hosts out of their positions and were obstructing the view of the others.

Herr Grossemann now spoke and cameras and pencils worked even more feverishly.

'It is a great pleasure for us to announce this new investment in the United Kingdom and I want to offer my company's thanks to Henry Morgan and his team at Concrete Hardening for all they have done to make our decision possible.'

'The UK motor industry has become a major customer for our products and it made sense to come here when it proved so difficult to expand our site at Dusseldorf.'

'We found ideal conditions in Concrete Hardening with a skilled workforce and plenty of space for future expansion . . .'

There were more serious and portentous comments of this kind which, it must be said, droned on just a little, although the audience in Concrete Hardening smiled with pleasure whilst three members of the audience in Dusseldorf, faces darkened in shame and fury, glared one at the other, and began wondering who could be blamed. This, as is well known, is the first consideration when something goes seriously wrong in public affairs in England.

They first rounded on the hapless Herr Becker who was beginning to look puzzled as he had already detected a change of mood in his guests.

'But we came all the way here to talk to you about getting the factory in Standing Stillbury – and you are announcing a move to Concrete Hardening. Couldn't you have told us first!?'

This time Herr Becker's eyes widened, with some surprise evident. 'What do you mean? We couldn't tell you before we made the public announcement, could we? It would have been, as I think you call it, a breach of confidence.'

But then, his brain catching up with the exact words used by Fred Meadows, a look of combined understanding and concern spread across Herr Becker's face.

'But . . . but you are saying you are here to talk about having the factory in your town!? We were told you just wanted to visit our factory. Lots of foreign groups do that – because we are supplying so many other countries.'

And then, a shade defensively, wondering if his own colleagues had made a dreadful mistake, 'We really didn't know this was your reason for coming – but please, wait a minute.'

The visitors were left fuming.

Chapter 15 – The End of the Road

Herr Becker returned quite quickly. He was most sympathetic. But he looked relieved.

'There really has been a misunderstanding. I have spoken with my colleague who arranged this visit and she says that there was no mention at all of the new factory. We were just asked for a visit. Do you have someone in your office called Miss Peefs?'

Three faces consulted each other, wordlessly, for just a second. The name wasn't pronounced quite correctly but there was no doubt about it. Two of the faces emitted an accusing 'Ah', pronounced very long, in connection with that name. The third face, that of Mr Muffle, didn't join them. He was beginning to realise that, in the rush to get back to the committee meeting, his instructions to Miss Peeves might have been less than full. This thought had been niggling away, at the back of his mind, for the past half-hour or so.

The Town Clerk took the initiative – as the Town Clerk usually has to when something has gone desperately wrong. The most articulate and forceful elected members usually shut up and leave things to the Town Clerk at moments like this.

'I'm afraid', he said gently to Herr Becker, 'that this is entirely my fault. I can only thank you for the generous hospitality you have shown us during a visit whose purpose was obviously confused.'

Now looking even more relieved – he really had been quite worried – Herr Becker offered assurances that the mistake was understood. 'These things', he consoled, 'happen from time to time in any organisation.' Privately he was wondering exactly what sort of organisation would let such a thing happen. But in his relief at the fault not lying with his own company, he felt strongly that this was a moment for generosity.

Mr Meadows, now regaining his composure (Jervis Boddington was close to frothing at the mouth as he considered explaining all this to the rest of the Conservative Club. He was quite beyond discussion for the moment.) added his apologies and asked Herr Becker an important question.

'Is there somewhere we could use for a few minutes to discuss this privately before we re-join our party?'

Herr Becker understood the significance of this question immediately. It would be vital to go back with the same story as the three were clearly identified as the architects of the whole affair – the worse for Councillor Boddington who had assumed his position from self-importance and pomposity rather than the conviction and duty which had more or less motivated the others.

'Yes – of course', he replied straight away. 'In these circumstances you can certainly use our Chairman's room – at the moment he is away in Eng . . .' The words froze as Herr Becker realised what he was about to say – so, without finishing the sentence, he just led them along the corridor to Herr Grossemann's office.

At the Town Hall in Standing Stillbury Miss Peeves thought she was having the difficult day. At the time of the great announcement of Concrete Hardening's success – a matter of national news importance – a local reporter with Radio Deepshire suddenly started thinking about a rumour he had just heard, and first dismissed as preposterous, that a deputation from Standing Stillbury had set off to the Zugswang Works in Germany.

He had telephoned the Town Hall and the absence of the Town Clerk, the Mayor and several other councillors he tried to contact at their home or work numbers got him thinking even more deeply.

So he called Miss Peeves and demanded to know where they all were. Miss Peeves, being unused to the ways of journalism, wasn't sure what to say, hesitated visibly (this is one of the few things than can come down a telephone line quite visibly, to a reporter at least) and then clammed-up with a statement that they were all on confidential business and that she could say no more. The word of the announcement at Concrete Hardening had also reached Miss Peeves by now and she began to feel uneasy as well as rattled by the reporter's questions.

The young reporter, for his part, began to smell a triumph which might launch a distinguished career. Lots of radio reports beginning with the stock words 'Red faced-officials were today explaining how . . .' or 'Audit chiefs grill Councillors . . .', and then newspaper articles crediting him with a major discovery of municipal scandal and incompetence. In this latter hope he was, of course, totally naive. All newspapers subsequently using the story would present it as if they, and they alone, had made the discovery. And in the scale of municipal scandal, this was more comedy than villainy.

In Herr Grossemann's office three worried looking envoys of Standing Stillbury Borough Council were thinking only of the immediate problem of explaining things to the rest of the party which was, by now, greatly enjoying the food and wine provided by Zugswang Components.

They considered the situation in silence for a few minutes. They stood beneath large oil-paintings of Herr Grossemann's grandfather and father, who glowered over them with expressions of sobriety and seriousness to match those of the past Chairmen of Deepshire County Council, similarly commemorated at the Shirehall at home. They might almost have been painted by the same artist.

The Mayor got straight to the nub of the issue.

'What the bloody hell do we tell that lot?'

Silence.

'Its a f—g outrage' – muttered several times by Jervis Boddington whose rate of recovery from disaster was not high. His face might have been mistaken for that of a bulldog chewing a wasp.

'We'll be crucified by the Planet and surcharged by the District bloody Auditor,' said Fred Meadows, whose brain was beginning to operate again.

Mr Muffle had thought about all these things and more. He looked weary and ashen.

'We can't put it off. We've just got to go and tell them. Then we've got to get them out of here and on the 'bus back to the hotel and then the airport.'

Another silence. But the statement was unanswerable. Any attempt to avoid the issue would make things much worse later.

The three shuffled, like condemned men, back along the corridor to the dining room.

The party had warmed up, the headaches from the previous night now quite out of mind. The catering staff had wondered at the amount of drink being consumed by what seemed to be business visitors but, on Herr Becker's instructions, had continued to pour on demand instead of easing back in that imperceptible way by which guests can usually be made to understand that things have gone far enough. So the men were talking more loudly, the woman (with two exceptions) a little more shrilly, and the food and especially the drink were disappearing a little faster. Everyone was enjoying it hugely, the purpose of the visit forgotten for the moment.

The Mayor, finding some reserves of moral courage in his adversity, led into the room ahead of the Town Clerk. Jervis Boddington was by now a long way behind.

Fred Meadows called for attention. It took a few minutes before his call penetrated all the befuddled brains before him. Finally it did.

They stopped talking and looked at him, some quizzically, some thinking that he was about to make the standard speech of thanks. But Herr Becker had by now withdrawn himself and the Zugswang catering staff from the room. He thought it more tactful. There were no Germans to thank.

'I have to tell you,' began the Mayor, 'that we have been to talk to our hosts privately . . .' (At this point some faces began to look excluded and indignant) 'and I'm afraid that it looks as if, for all our efforts,' (he began to find words which, with his customary skill were honest enough without being totally clear), 'we are not going to get Zugswang Components in Standing Stillbury.' (The more indignant expressions softened.)

'In fact', he went on, 'the Company have explained to us that, for reasons of confidentiality, they were quite unable to tell us before today that the decision has already been taken in favour of Concrete Hardening.'

'It has even', he continued, 'been announced in Deep-shire this morning – a fact which has made it possible for them to tell us the situation now.'

'The Company', he added, his natural flow and assurance returning with each sentence, 'has offered its sincere apologies for having to hold back this information, because of problems with their competitors, and expresses the hope that you will all understand their difficulty.'

This last was, of course, a direct lie – but a fairly safe one which Zugswang Components would only contest if forced by some attack upon themselves.

Mr Muffle looked at the floor.

From the back of the room a burp escaped noisily from the silence. A voice mumbled, 'The bastards.' Another complained 'They don't bloody change, do they?' Someone else giggled.

But no-one was sure what else to say – so Fred Meadows acted on the instinct that action, any action, was best.

'I'm afraid that we have to get back to the coach now to pick up our things from the hotel and then get back to the airport – do please get on board as quickly as possible.'

It was 3.15 pm. They filed out, the glee all gone. When they reached the foyer, and wandered out, the weather had changed. It was raining heavily, so much so that the water was bouncing back a few inches from the roadway. The outlook was suddenly rather poor.

The driver of their coach had been told that the party would be out by no later than 3.00 pm. Herr Becker, most unusually for him, had omitted to tell him that the visit would be going on a little longer, all things considered. The driver wasn't a typical German who did everything to the second, according to plan. He had waited for 14 minutes 30 seconds before deciding that the British weren't coming any more and he had to be at his next job.

As the visitors drifted into the rainy landcsape they could see just far enough through the murk to make out the disappearing rear lights. They waved frantically and shouted loudly, but were not seen. Standing Stillbury had missed the bus.

Back in England, the happiness of Concrete Hardening

had been tempered by great unhappiness just a few miles away in the County Town where, coincidentally, it was also raining.

Blanks Bearings was closing down.

The announcement was made suddenly at 2.30 pm without there having been any prior warning whatsoever. The Company's escalating losses made it no longer viable and it was being closed to reduce the damage to the shareholders. Sir Blathwell Scam wasn't there to tell the employees. Neither was the Personnel Manager. They were both at a meeting in London at which they were ensuring that their own financial positions were preserved amidst the ruins of the decades-old enterprise. They and the shareholders would be saved by a plan, still very secret, to demolish the offices and factories and re-develop the site for housing, a vast superstore and a very expensive residential home for old people – all managed by a new and totally separate company with no obligations to the old workforce.

The announcement was made by letter. Photo-copied letters were handed to the employees, all 2,000 of them. They were handed round by glum office staff – some of whom, in order to do this, had to enter the factory sheds for the first time. The letters began with the words 'Dear Sir or Madam' and bore no signature at the bottom. They were all redundant with immediate effect and there might not be enough money available to pay the normal redundancy terms. So the Government redundancy scheme might have to be brought in – for what that was worth to a man with a large mortgage and 25 years of his life suddenly up in smoke.

After a while, long lines of sad and angry-looking people began to march away from Blanks Bearings for the last time. One or two wept in their shock and dismay. They gradually disappeared into a gloomy townscape, overcast by heavy clouds from which rain continued to pour. Just a few were thinking about writing to the new German Company which was supposed to be setting up at Concrete Hardening. About a quarter of those who had this thought would get around to doing it.

Standing Stillbury's small rate of unemployment had

doubled between the hours of two and three on a wet Wednesday afternoon. The Town Forum would meet a few weeks later to discuss the social implications at enormous length.

The social implications would include the re-possession of houses as mortgage payments were missed, the loss of motor cars bought on credit and, with that, a complete inability to find work beyond the immediate neighbourhood. There would be poverty both at home and, for those with children at college or dependant elderly relatives, further afield.

Marriages would break up under the stress of penury in an economy in which decent jobs were harder and harder to find and those which could be found were low-paid and prone to evaporate like snow-flakes in May.

But, through all of that, Standing Stillbury would remain a very nice town, quite unspoiled by change.